"I need a woman to pretend she's my mistress. You'd have to act the part, dress the part and convince people that we're lovers."

"We are talking…fake mistress here?"

"Do you really think that I need to pay for sex?"

"How would I know? I don't have rich Sicilian tycoons offering me the moon just to pretend to be their mistresses every day, do I?" Misty snapped out in bewilderment and embarrassment.

"And if you take that tone and attitude, you are unlikely to have even one Sicilian tycoon still interested."

Dear Reader,

Last year I read a touching newspaper story about two sisters who had been separated as children and then reunited as adults. That article sparked off the idea for this trilogy. Broken relationships and adoption can lead to siblings losing touch with each other through no choice of their own.

Each book deals with the different life experience of three sisters and the men they love: Freddy, who has initially no idea that she has sisters, Misty, who grows up in care, and Ione, who was adopted.

As you'll find out through reading this series, their mother actually made a second marriage. Could it be that there are more stories to come?

Lynne Graham

Lynne Graham

THE DISOBEDIENT MISTRESS

SISTER BRIDES

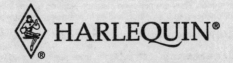

HARLEQUIN®

TORONTO • NEW YORK • LONDON
AMSTERDAM • PARIS • SYDNEY • HAMBURG
STOCKHOLM • ATHENS • TOKYO • MILAN • MADRID
PRAGUE • WARSAW • BUDAPEST • AUCKLAND

ISBN 0-373-12277-2

THE DISOBEDIENT MISTRESS

First North American Publication 2002.

CHAPTER ONE

LEONE ANDRACCHI lounged back in his comfortable leather chair and surveyed the woman whom he would use as a weapon in his quest for revenge.

Across the busy room, Misty Carlton was keeping her catering staff hard at work dispensing refreshments. She wore her copper hair in a no-nonsense style. Her grey suit and sensible shoes were neither feminine nor flattering and her pale face was unadorned by make-up. Her whole appearance suggested a businesslike and serious young woman keen not to draw attention to her sex, and her cover seemed to work for Leone had yet to see a single one of his executives attempt to flirt with her.

Was every man in the room with the exception of himself blind? Did only *he* see the promise of those silvergrey eyes and the voluptuous fullness of that lush pink mouth? Dressed in appropriate clothing, she would be stunning, far more arresting than any conventional beauty for her colouring gave her a fey, sensual quality that was unusual. He was already picturing her slender curves embellished by silk lingerie and her long, slim, coltish legs sheathed in cobweb-fine stockings and complemented by very high heels. She was tall but he was taller still and she would not need to wear flat shoes around him. A selfmocking smile lurked in the depths of Leone's dark-asnight eyes as he conceded that he had yet to mentally clothe her beyond the level of her undergarments. But then he was a Sicilian to the backbone and all Sicilian men knew how to truly appreciate an attractive woman.

Within a couple of weeks at most, Misty Carlton would

be one of the most talked-about women in London. As his mistress, she'd find her name would hit the gossip columns and the paparazzi would go digging into her background and if their quest was inefficient, he would ensure that a tip was dropped in the right quarter. Having established her identity to his own satisfaction, he had left the revealing links in place. Indeed, everything that would happen in the near future had been decided almost six months earlier when he had first found her and worked out how best to lure her into the position of a sitting duck waiting for him to take aim and fire. Which was right where she was at this particular moment, Leone savoured.

Misty Carlton was the illegitimate daughter of the man against whom Leone had sworn vengeance in his sister's name: Oliver Sargent. The smooth-talking politician, who had founded his reputation as a respectable family man by preaching moral standards and who lived an exceedingly nice life on his inherited wealth. Oliver Sargent, who was a hypocrite, a seducer of teenagers and ultimately little better than a murderer. Oliver Sargent, who had left Battista to die alone in the shattered remnants of her car sooner than call the emergency services and risk a scandal.

Leone's dark, chiselled face was sombre. Though it was almost a year since his sister's funeral, Leone's gut still twisted with pain whenever he allowed himself to remember how Battista's life had been wilfully, cruelly and mercilessly sacrificed. The doctors had told him that had she been discovered sooner she might have survived the crash. That summer, she had only been nineteen years old, a politics student doing research work on Sargent's staff.

A beautiful, idealistic girl with bright brown eyes, long black curly hair and a very trusting nature. Within weeks of her beginning her volunteer placement, Leone had been heartily sick of the sound of Sargent's name but it had not occurred to him that a bad case of hero worship might put

Battista at risk. After all, Oliver Sargent was a married man and a quarter of a century older than his kid sister. He had overlooked the fact that Sargent was a handsome charmer, who could easily pass for being a great deal younger than he actually was.

'Mr Andracchi...?'

Unaware of quite how intimidating his grim expression was, Leone focused in some surprise on the pastries being offered to him, for the almond biscuits and custard tarts were traditional Sicilian treats. The slender hand holding the plate was shaking almost imperceptibly but his gaze was keen. He glanced up into Misty Carlton's drawn face, recognising the marks of strain there in the bluish shadows beneath her eyes and the tense set of her delicate jawbone. She had brown lashes as long as a child's and she was trembling. But then she was desperate. He *knew* that for he had planned it that way. She was on the very brink of losing the business that she had worked so hard to build up. He held her in the palm of his hand.

'Thank you,' Leone murmured, dark deep drawl rather mocking for if she fondly imagined that he was likely to be impressed by so unsubtle an attempt at downright flattery, she was very much mistaken. Contracts were awarded on the basis of price, efficiency and reliability and, whether she liked it or not and through no fault of his, she had broken more than one of the basic rules of setting up a new business. '*Nucatoli* and *pasta ciotti*. What a pleasant surprise. You are spoiling me.'

A tiny betraying pulse was flickering like mad just below her fragile collar-bone, drawing his attention to the fine, delicate skin of her throat. 'I like to experiment...that's all,' Misty said breathlessly.

She was all of a quiver and her body language screamed at him: the dilated dark pupils, the flush on her cheeks, the moist pink of her parted lips. He turned her on and, had he not known what he *did* know about her, he might have believed that she was too innocent to hide those sexual signals of availability. But he knew better, felt free to assume that, had the room been empty, he might have pulled her down onto his lap and explored that quivering, slender body so hot and eager for his with her willing encouragement. His own sex threatened to betray him with primitive male urgency but he thought about revenge instead and his blood cooled fast. He had no intention of bedding Oliver Sargent's daughter. She would be his mistress in name only.

'Don't we all?' Leone quipped with husky suggestiveness and bit into a tiny custard tart that melted in his mouth, while she hovered like a submissive handmaiden to one side of him. A faint sardonic smile curved his masculine lips. He liked her stance. He was an old-fashioned guy and the pastry was delicious. Maybe in her spare time she would be able to occupy herself in his kitchen. Eager to please, she certainly was. Though someone ought to have warned her that even a hint of nervous desperation was likely to alert clients to an unsound business.

'It's good,' Leone told her softly.

The big silver-grey eyes lit up with a surge of relief and pride. He had an erotic image of her spread across his bed in the drowsing heat of a Sicilian afternoon, glorious red hair cascading in a tangle, lush pink mouth begging for his while she writhed and moaned with pleasure beneath his expert hands. Sadly, it was not to be, he reminded himself, exasperated by the predictable effects of his own powerful libido.

She poured his coffee with her own hands. He wondered if her rock-star lover had appreciated those little touches of essential femininity calculated to make even the wimpiest male feel as though he could go out and club a lion to death before dragging it back to the connubial cave to impress her in turn. She was no fragile little flower, though. The file on her had turned up quite a few surprises for she might be only twenty-two, but she had led a chequered life and one that might have inspired his compassion had she not, it seemed, been guilty of fleecing a little old lady out of her savings. Behind those mist-coloured eyes lurked a greedy little schemer with a heart of stone.

Blood will out, Leone thought fatalistically as he accepted the coffee already sugared to his preference. She might not have the foggiest idea of who her father was and she might never have met him but he already saw a similarity between Oliver Sargent and his natural daughter in the way that she seemed to use people and reinvent herself to turn situations to her own advantage.

Melissa Carlton had grown up in a series of foster homes and trouble seemed to follow her around. She had once been engaged to a prosperous landowner and her former fiancé's mother was *still* congratulating herself on her success in seeing off a young woman whom she had deemed to be both mercenary and calculating. The rock-star lover had followed: an unwashed-looking yob with spiky bleach-blond hair given to screaming indecipherable lyrics into microphones while Misty had danced wildly on one side of the stage. That had not lasted long either.

'May I have a word with you, Mr Andracchi?' Misty asked tautly.

'Not just at present,' Leone said, watching her flinch and pale without an ounce of remorse.

She could stew a little longer. And why not? Ultimately, she was going to get the deal of the century and profit very nicely indeed from their arrangement. Saving her skin stuck in his throat but what else could he do? She was Oliver Sargent's Achilles heel and he needed her co-operation to bring the bastard down. Not that she would know how she was helping him until it was too late. But then even the best deals came at a price and she was not a sensitive woman. Sensitive women did not rip off old ladies and leave them struggling to make ends meet while continuing to pose as a caring pseudo-daughter.

When the press identified Misty Carlton as Sargent's illegitimate child, her father's political career would go down the tubes for no man had been more sanctimonious about his moral principles than Oliver Sargent. His good-living childless wife might well pull the plug on him too but Leone had no interest in that possibility. He already knew what Sargent valued most: his power, his ambitious hopes of higher office in government, his adoring coterie of female supporters. And when the scandal broke, Oliver Sargent was going to be stripped bare of his pride and his power and his influence. It would be a brutal punishment for a man who revelled in his own importance and lived for admiration. Once Sargent's cover was blown all the other dirt would eventually surface too: his financial double-dealing and questionable friendships with dishonest businessmen. He would be ruined beyond all hope of political recovery.

It wasn't enough, though, it wasn't nearly enough to compensate for Battista's sweet life cut off in its prime, but when the axe fell Leone would be sure to let his victim know *why* he had destroyed him. Sargent was already nervous around him although the older man did not yet suspect that Leone knew that he had been in that car the night his kid sister had died. But then Battista's sleazy seducer had covered his tracks too well and, no matter how hard Leone had tried, proof of that fact had been impossible to obtain.

He watched Misty Carlton, who was the very picture of her late mother, marshal her staff. Unless he was very much mistaken, Oliver Sargent would begin sweating and fearing exposure the very *instant* he saw her and heard her name…

Misty wondered if she had ever hated anyone as much as she hated Leone Andracchi.

He had dismissed her as though she were a servant speaking up out of turn but this was the last day but one of her temporary contract and she had yet to be told whether or not it was going to be renewed for the next year. If it wasn't, she would be bankrupted. Perspiration beading her short upper lip, Misty got on with her work but, no matter where she was in the gracious room with its oppressive clubby male atmosphere, she was conscious of Leone Andracchi's brooding presence.

A real Sicilian tycoon, fabulously wealthy and famously devious and unpredictable to deal with. He dominated the room like a big black storm cloud within which lurked the threat of a lightning strike. His own executives were nervous as cats around him, eager to defer to him, keen to impress, paling if he even began to frown. Yet he was only thirty years old, young indeed to wield such enormous power. But then he was supposed to be absolutely brilliant in business.

Shame about the personality, Misty thought bitterly. It was just her luck that she should be forced to kowtow to a sexist dinosaur, who had taken her attentions quite as his due. My goodness, he had *loved* it when she'd brought him those special pastries and had practically purred like a jungle cat while she'd sugared his blasted coffee for him. Her strong pride had stung with every obsequious move, for boot-licking did not come naturally to her. Perhaps the Sicilian baking had been overkill but, really, what did she have left to lose? Beggars couldn't be choosers. She had crawled for Birdie's sake, Birdie who was going to lose her home if Misty didn't manage to pull her own irons out of the fire and get that contract confirmed. And when it came to Birdie, there was no limit to the efforts Misty was willing to make.

'That Andracchi guy is *so* gorgeous,' her friend and employee, Clarice, groaned in a die-away voice as she stacked cups into containers by Misty's side. 'Every time I look at him I feel like I've just died and gone to heaven.'

'Shh.' Misty reddened with annoyance, for a waitress casting languishing lustful glances at the big chief would hardly qualify as professional behaviour.

'You're always looking at him out of the corner of your eye,' the chirpy and curvaceous brunette whispered back cheekily before she walked away.

All right, so she looked, but not because she was a mug for those serious dark good looks of his! No, she looked the way one looked to check a lion was still in a cage with the door safely locked. Leone Andracchi unnerved her. It had to be her imagination that she felt that *he* was always watching *her* for she had yet to catch those brooding dark golden eyes doing so, but in his radius she felt hideously self-conscious.

And yet in any normal business empire the size of Andracchi Industries, she would never even have got to meet a male as hugely important as Leone Andracchi. After all, she was only a caterer on a short trial contract to just *one* of his companies and surely far beneath his lofty notice. Furthermore, Brewsters was not in London but based on the outskirts of a country town in Norfolk. Yet, on a visit to Brewsters, Leone Andracchi had taken the trouble to interview her personally. He had also sent her jumping through a line of mental hoops like a circus animal he was training for his own nasty amusement.

As her wan face stiffened at the recollection, she scolded herself for the resentment that lingered. In accepting her bid for the contract and very much surprising her in so doing, Leone Andracchi had given her what had seemed to be the opportunity of a lifetime. It was hardly his fault that that opportunity had turned sour or that she had bitten off more than she could chew.

'Andracchi is what I call a *real* man,' Clarice stressed in a feeling sigh of infuriating appreciation as she shoved past again. 'All muscles and rampant energy. He just reeks of sex in the raw. You know he'd be a wicked fantasy in bed—'

'He has love rat written all over him and a lousy reputation with women!' Misty gritted in a driven undertone. 'Will you *please* drop the subject?'

'I was only trying to give you a laugh.' Her friend pulled a surprised grimace. 'Lighten up, Misty.'

Feeling guilty, Misty reddened, aware her nerves were jumping like electrified beans. But even her friend had no idea just how precarious her business, Carlton Catering, had become. It was ready to crash and go to the wall. If she did not get that all important contract from Andracchi Industries, the bank would refuse to extend her loan and she would not even have sufficient funds left to pay her employees at the end of the month, never mind her suppliers. Shame drenched her in a tidal wave. How had she got into such a mess?

A blond male in a smart suit approached her. 'Mr Andracchi will see you now in his office.'

She could see the man's barely concealed surprise that Leone Andracchi should be involving himself yet again in such a minor matter. But then as the great man himself had drawled in explanation almost four months earlier, 'Lunch is an art to a Sicilian and I want the executives here to benefit from a new experience. I'm tired of watching people scoff sandwiches at their desks. I believe that a proper meal will increase productivity throughout the afternoon.'

So every day she had provided a light lunch in the executive dining room that had been set up and on afternoons like this, when a major business powwow concluded, she had been asked to stay on to serve refreshments as well. Visiting the cloakroom first, she washed her hands and checked that she was still tidy. She wasn't looking her best and she knew it, which didn't help. Sleepless nights and constant worry had left their mark.

Her own fault, she told herself bitterly. She had taken a risk on Leone Andracchi's whim and on what might yet prove to be an experiment he had no intention of even continuing. Furthermore, even if he had decided to retain the lunches, there was no guarantee whatsoever that her business would win the contract. He was going to kiss her off. She knew it, could *feel* it in her bones. Her punishment for borrowing from the bank to expand was coming. What was it to him if her piffling little firm went into receivership? He would probably like to see her beg. Could she do it for Birdie? Beg that big, muscle-bound, arrogant jerk for mercy? She shuddered at the prospect but her only alternative was even less appetizing: Flash would haul her out of trouble without hesitation. Only it would be for a price this time and the price would be her body and she hoped to heaven that she would never, ever sink that low…

A secretary who looked suitably cowed by the effect of a week-long visit from the tycoon boss of Andracchi Industries opened the door of a big office for her. Straightening her slight shoulders, Misty breathed in deep and walked in, striving for a look of calm confidence, which was in no way echoed by her churning tummy and her damp palms. Please, please don't let him try to shake hands, she prayed inwardly.

'Sit down, Miss Carlton.'

Leone Andracchi was on the phone, standing by the sunlit windows of the spacious office. She listened to him talking in soft, liquid Italian, the way a real smoothie talked to a lover. Phone sex, sleazebag, Misty thought loftily and her upper lip curled in disgust. But, unfortunately, Clarice was right on one score. He *was* drop-dead fantastic to look at. Luxuriant black hair that just begged to be disarranged by a woman's fingers, stunning high cheekbones, stunning everything, really, she conceded grudgingly. Classic arrogant nose, well-defined ebony brows, really masculine strong jaw, beautifully shaped mouth. As for the eyes, those eyes of his were a revelation on their own. Black as pitch in certain moods, all lustrous, dazzling, sexy gold in another. And he knew how to use them all right to signify just about everything that other people used words to convey.

She had seen those eyes, in bully mode, freeze employees in their tracks. Send female office staff fluttering with the same sense of threat as hens scenting a fox. He got off on women fussing round him. He was the 'Me Tarzan, you Jane' type and he went for fluffy busty little blondes who giggled and gasped and clung. Pathetic, really. In her opinion, a *real* man would have wanted a *real* woman, one with a brain, one capable of fighting back and putting him in his place. And if ever a guy had needed putting in his place, it was Leone Andracchi. He was so full of himself he set her teeth on edge.

Finishing his call, Leone flicked a glance at his waiting victim, wondered why she had that curious little scornful smile hovering on her lips and that faraway, almost smug look in her eyes. He strolled with fluid grace over to the desk and realised that she was genuinely miles away, one of those individuals whose imagination was strong enough to blank out all sense of time and surroundings.

Misty was acquainted with that old chestnut about imagining intimidating people naked to bring them down to human size, only she wasn't even a little tempted to picture Leone Andracchi shorn of his exquisitely tailored suit. But just as suddenly she was seeing Leone Andracchi in her mind's eye and her mind had developed a dismaying life all of its own, imagination running riot on that tall, well-built physique of his. Her own embarrassing thoughts shocked her rigid, shocked her right back to awareness again, cheeks hot, skin tight over her bones.

'Welcome back, Miss Carlton,' Leone Andracchi murmured with sardonic bite.

'Mr Andracchi…' Heart beating so fast, she felt as if it were banging at the foot of her throat, Misty forced herself to raise her head high.

'I'm sorry I kept you waiting,' he added.

No, he wasn't. She didn't know how she knew that, for that lean dark angel face was uniquely uninformative, but she sensed it. He lounged back in galling relaxation against the desk, the indolent angle of his sleek, taut, muscular frame pronounced. He had to be about six feet four at least, she calculated, and not for the first time.

'Naturally you want to know my thoughts on the contract due to be awarded. Although I'm really not obligated to give you that information,' Leone Andracchi pointed out smoothly. 'However, in the light of the excellent standard of service you have pioneered over the past eight weeks, I feel it's only fair to tell you *why* your bid has been unsuccessful.'

Her tummy flipped at the confirmation of the refusal that she had most feared. The blood drained from her set features and her hands laced together on her lap. 'I don't need empty compliments,' she said tightly. 'If Carlton Catering hasn't been awarded the contract, then you obviously weren't satisfied with the service at all.'

'It's not that simple,' Leone drawled. 'You're overextended and it would be very unwise to take the risk that your business will stay afloat for the duration of a year long agreement.'

Her silvery grey eyes were now widened to their fullest extent. For the first time she ditched her caution and connected direct with his brilliant dark golden eyes. 'May I ask you where you received that information?'

'My sources are private.'

Meeting that steady, fathomless gaze, she could feel her head beginning to swim and the breath catching in her throat. 'It's quite untrue.'

'Don't lie to me. I have no time for lies,' Leone told her smoothly. 'My information is always accurate. I know that the only way your bank will extend your loan is if you bring them the contract for the next year's catering here signed, sealed and delivered.'

'If someone at the bank has been making allegations about the viability of my business, I will be sure to make an official complaint.' Misty threw her head back, silver eyes blazing challenge. 'I assure you that were you to give me that contract I would deliver the service required for the period specified and I would not have any problems in doing so.'

'I'm impressed by your optimism,' Leone countered levelly, 'but let's cut to the chase. You have talent and you're great at organisation but you fell down when it came to the bid for the first contract. Your price was ludicrously low. Yet you're in a labour-intensive industry, saddled with high staff turnover, crippling insurance costs and public health regulations that are very expensive for a small business to meet. As a result, you have barely recouped your costs.'

'I wanted the job. I priced that bid to win in the obvious hope of recouping costs over the next year,' Misty informed him. 'You said you liked to support new local businesses—'

'Not when the captain at the helm is a woman who refuses to acknowledge when she's in over her head. How you can sit there and argue with me when I know for a fact that you're behind with the rent on your business premises, behind with your bank loan *and* up to your pretty throat in debt—'

'Leave my throat…pretty or otherwise…out of this, please.' Misty rose to her feet, no longer able to tolerate being looked down on by him. How dared he speak to her in such a way? How *dared* he? It was bad enough learning that the contract on which she had placed all her hopes was to be awarded elsewhere, but that he should add insult to injury by enumerating what he deemed to be her mistakes was more than flesh and blood could bear.

'And losing your temper with me will impress me even less,' Leone informed her with a derisive look at her aggressive stance. She might be around five feet ten tall, but she was as slender as a willow wand. What on earth was the matter with her? She was useless at bluffing. Her eyes gave her away every time. Did she really expect him to waste time listening to her trying to convince him that she *wasn't* on the edge of a financial abyss?

In the space of a second, rage almost ate Misty alive. The temper that she had long since mastered threatened to overflow like lava. She wanted to take a swing at him. She wanted to wipe that derisive slant off his lean, strong face with a well-placed fist and that simple awareness disconcerted her enough to put a brake on her anger.

'You've brought me in here, given me the bad news, but you *didn't* need to personalise the issue,' Misty stated with curt dignity. 'So why would you think I want to impress you now?'

An ebony brow elevated. 'I could be thinking of throwing you a lifeline.'

A shaken and involuntary laugh escaped Misty. She was

grateful that he had not given her an opening in which to beg. She was even grateful that he had made her furious. For if she were forced to stop and consider the appalling consequences of losing that contract, she might well come apart at the seams and embarrass herself. He liked playing games with people, she decided. Or maybe it was only women he liked toying with.

'Is that really a possibility?' The tip of her tongue came out to moisten her dry lower lip as she wondered if it was remotely likely that, in spite of what he had so far said about her business acumen, he might have some other job to offer her.

The silence hummed like a circular saw on her straining nerves. His attention had dropped to her lips, the too wide, too full mouth she hated. No doubt he was noticing that it was out of proportion to her face. Men were supposed to think about sex, what was it…at least once every five minutes? She reckoned he would be challenged to keep his mind clean for sixty seconds. He had an aura of potent virility that no woman could avoid noticing. She studied him, the lush black lashes screening his gleaming scrutiny, and her lips actually tingled with her awareness of him, her rebellious body stirring with the sensations she had grown to fiercely resent experiencing in his vicinity. The sudden tense, full sensation lifting her breasts inside her cotton bra cups, the utterly demeaning throb of her nipples tightening.

Never had Misty been so grateful for the concealment of her jacket. Imagine him *seeing* that physical evidence, imagine him *knowing* that he could make her stupid body react like that with one charged glance! Ever since she had met him, she had recognised that cruel Old Mother nature was reminding her that she had hormones, but it meant nothing. She had been hurt too much to risk herself again with any man and she need hardly worry that this particular male was likely to make a pass, for Leone Andracchi was just doing what came naturally to a sexual animal of his appetites: considering every passing woman of a certain age on her merits. And she knew her merits to be few and far between.

'Anything's possible. Didn't anyone ever tell you that?' Leone murmured, smooth as velvet.

Flash had told her that when he'd been trying to talk her into his bed. Try it, you might find you like it. *Not* the seduction line of the century, but another week or two of his determined siege and she might have succumbed out of gratitude and love, for she did love him, would always love him, only not the way he had wanted her to love him. But sometimes in low moments she would think that she should have snatched at his offer and made the best of it.

'It's my motto.' Misty was careful to keep Leone Andracchi out of focus, determined to blank him out as a man, get her foolish physical self back under control and let those taunting sensations subside.

'Sit down,' Leone Andracchi told her.

Obviously *something* was in the offing. She dropped back down into the seat, thought that maybe, after all, it had been worth staying up half the night to produce those wretched Sicilian recipes for his benefit. Major egos liked being stroked. Honey went far further than vinegar, she reminded herself doggedly. What had happened to her belief that she could make herself beg? Why did the prospect of speaking even one humble word to Leone Andracchi clog up her throat like a threatened dose of poison?

'I have a role that I would like you to fulfil for me over the next two months.' Leone surveyed her steadily. 'In return I would rescue your business, and at the end of our agreement I would ensure that you had sufficent work to survive. What do you think?'

'The last time I looked there wasn't two blue moons hanging out there in that sky,' Misty quipped with helpless bluntness.

CHAPTER TWO

LEONE ANDRACCHI dealt Misty a look of hauteur, his wide mouth tightening with perceptible exasperation.

Having immediately recognised her mistake in making such a facetious response, Misty had turned hot pink with discomfiture. She could not work out where those inappropriate words of doubt had emerged from. It was the effect of *him* again, she decided. He spooked her, put her on edge, knocked her out of the cautious business mode which she had no problem maintaining around other clients.

'I'm sorry,' Misty said flatly, 'but what you just said sounded too good to be true.'

'So you're now willing to concede that you're facing bankruptcy?' Leone probed.

A chill at the very sound of that terrifying word sank into Misty's bones and she shifted uneasily in her chair. 'Mr Andracchi—'

'Until you admit that reality, I will go no further,' he warned her.

Her earlier argument to the contrary had evidently offended. She would have loved to have known what he would have done in the same position. Announced to his one last hope that his back was up against the wall? No way, he was far too clever for that, so why was he judging her for her attempt to regain his confidence? Just because he refused to credit that she could have fulfilled that contract for a year! But she *knew* she could have, had done the figures over and over again, had been ready to go on living like a church mouse to have done so.

'Or leave my office,' Leone Andracchi added with lethal cool.

'I'm…facing…bankruptcy,' Misty framed like a clockwork toy with a battery about to run flat. The admission hurt, made real what she had until then refused to contemplate and she hated him all the more for forcing her to that brink.

'Thank you. As I said I have a promising proposition to offer you. It's nothing to do with catering, although if you find yourself overcome with the urge to cook Sicilian cuisine in your spare time, I will have no objection,' Leone imparted with a sardonic smile.

The offer had nothing to do with catering? *Nothing?* She hoped that swallowing his sarcasm in silence would prove to be worth her while.

'First, I want your assurance that nothing I now say will be repeated beyond this office.'

Since the first rule of any business was respecting client confidentiality, Misty bridled at that statement. 'Of course. I'm no gossip and I'd be a fool if I was.'

'I need a woman to pretend that she's my mistress.'

She heard an imaginary crash as her jaw metaphorically hit the floor. She waited on the punchline, certain he was mocking her in some way and determined not to rise prematurely to the bait.

'You will note that word, "pretend,"'Leone Andracchi stressed with unblemished cool. 'I'm not into sexual harassment of my employees and you would be, in effect, my employee for I would insist that you signed a legal agreement to maintain the fiction until *I* say that your role is at an end.'

Misty sucked in a ragged breath and continued to stare at him, utterly silenced by that second speech. He was actually serious, yet she could not credit that he was addressing her with such an offer. What reason could he have for asking *any* woman to pretend to be his mistress? He had to have a little black book the size of an entire library. For goodness' sake, wasn't he dating an actress from a television show at present? Jassy something or other? A pneumatic blonde with the kind of curves that even other women stole a shaken second glance at?

'I'm afraid I don't understand,' Misty framed very slowly and succinctly while she wondered if he were a brick short of the full load in the mental department or drunk as a skunk and just not showing physical signs of his condition.

'You're not required to understand. I have my own reasons and I don't intend to share them. I know women don't like mysteries but, in this case, discretion is necessary.'

'If you do have some…er…need to hire a woman for such a novel role, I can't think why you should approach me,' Misty reasoned with enormous care.

'Can't you?' A faint smile momentarily softened the tough line of his mouth.

She had no intention of lowering herself to the level of spelling out the obvious. But she wasn't beautiful or glamorous, nor did she have the high public profile of the kind of women he was usually associated with.

'Is this some kind of a joke?'

'It's on the level.'

'But you must know hundreds of women,' Misty protested, intimidated by his persistence. 'Why me?'

'I prefer to hire and fire rather than coax and trust,' Leone countered without hesitation. 'Why are you trying to dissuade me from rescuing you from your financial problems?'

Put like that, keeping quiet seemed more sensible, but she could not accept that he was serious without some idea of his motivation for such a weird offer. 'This is very strange.'

Leone shrugged a broad shoulder in unconcerned acknowledgement.

'I mean...*seriously*,' Misty emphasised.

'I am serious and the position wouldn't be that easy to fill. You'd have to act the part, dress the part and convince people that we're lovers.'

Warm colour inched up beneath her fine complexion and she glanced away from her studious scrutiny of his exquisitely tailored suit jacket. 'I don't think I'd be a great hit in that department.'

'You just need the right props and the ability to do exactly as I tell you at all times. It would definitely be a case of when I say jump...you say how high?'

Misty could see herself being a major disappointment in that field too. But it was dawning on her that, peculiar as his proposition was, he was not pulling her leg. He wanted a fake mistress. What did being a fake mistress entail?

'We are talking....*fake* mistress here?' Misty prompted in a strained undertone.

'Do you really think that I need to pay for sex?'

Her even white teeth gritted. If she said jump to him and he said how high, she would direct him to the nearest lift shaft, but with that ego of his he would bounce back out of the fall. 'There's no need to get that personal, Mr Andracchi. Your private life is your business but my safety is mine.'

'Are you trying to suggest that I might be some sort of pervert?' Leone shot back at her in an incredulous growl.

'How would I know? This is not a common or garden offer. Like, I don't have rich Sicilian tycoons offering me the moon just to pretend to be their mistresses every day, do I?' Misty snapped out in bewilderment and embarrassment.

'And if you take that tone and attitude, you are unlikely to have even *one* Sicilian tycoon still interested.'

Legs cramped by the rigidity of her posture in the chair, Misty got up again and walked across the office before spinning round to face him, wide grey eyes frowning. 'Just tell me why you're asking me to do this…why me?'

'You couldn't afford to welch on any deal we would make or change the terms to suit yourself.' He stood straight and tall, eyes hard gold and direct.

Misty flinched. Mr Mean and Tough, who, it seemed, knew exactly how she was placed and that was between a rock and a hard place. He had no shame about reminding her of that unpalatable fact. Perhaps it was a timely reminder too. Any alternative to bankruptcy and Birdie losing her home ought to be considered. But how could she possibly consider taking on a role in which she would be less than convincing? Didn't he see that? People wouldn't believe that she was his mistress for one minute! He specialised in beautiful women. Yes, he liked women, but why did she judge him for that?

'I couldn't do it…' she muttered. 'We mix like oil and water. I wouldn't be at home in the sort of social life you must have. And I couldn't possibly convince anyone that we were…lovers.'

'Oh, I think you underestimate yourself on that score,' Leone breathed in a different timbre, rich, dark drawl snaking round her like a husky, mesmeric spell.

Nibbling at the soft underside of her full lower lip, Misty was entrapped by the intensity of his narrowed golden stare. Gorgeous eyes, undeniably gorgeous eyes. Her mouth ran dry, her muscles tightening in response. Even his voice, liquid dark enticement of the most dangerous kind, yet another enhancement to his magnetic masculine presence. The gene pool had not been stingy when he'd been born.

Entirely against her own will, she wanted to smile, soften, be a woman in all the ways she had once allowed herself to be even if it put her at risk of getting hurt again. The atmosphere was buzzing with the sensual vibes he could put out. He could whip up the tension without effort. And no matter how hard she tried to remain impervious, excitement nibbled at her every nerve ending and she quivered as a taunting flame lit low in her pelvis and forced her to press her thighs together in shamed disconcertion.

'Just say the word and sign on the dotted line and all your troubles are at an end.'

'What would playing your pretend mistress involve?' Misty heard herself ask and surprised herself.

'Living in the apartment I would supply, wearing the clothes I buy, going where I ask when I ask without question.'

Mistress as in mindless *slave*, she translated with a secret little shard of amusement. He was a real domineering louse. But it was interesting to note that he wasn't suggesting any type of shared accommodation. The masquerade would only be of the public variety and would require no greater intimacy. He wanted a dressed-up doll to play a stupid role for some reason he refused to reveal. Maybe it was another Andracchi whim like the executive lunches. Or maybe it had some business purpose…which would make it an unusual job but still a job like any other.

It wasn't as though he would be expecting her to hop into bed with him. Of course, he wouldn't. Her face burned that she had even suspected he might. After all, he had much more attractive possibilities than her available: women who had probably forgotten more than she had even learned about bedroom pursuits. She would be as safe as houses with him but she would be selling herself, handing over her pride and her independence in return for cold hard cash support. That was cheap and nasty and the thought of it left an unpleasant taste in her mouth, but she had Birdie and her employees to think about and pride didn't pay the bills.

'What would you do for me?' she whispered chokily, the humiliating request for greater clarity on that point hurting her.

'Settle your debts, put your business back on an even keel, cover the wages of your staff while you're working for me. Anything else, name it. I'm prepared to negotiate.' Leone Andracchi gazed back at her, cool as ice.

Her tummy churned. She loathed him for issuing that unvarnished bribe of greater remuneration. He had it all worked out. He believed that he could buy her and it shamed her to acknowledge that she had put herself in a position where he could think that and act on it.

'I'll think it over this evening.' That admission cut through Misty's pride like the first wounding slash of a knife.

'What do you have to think over?'

'I think you're underestimating my side of what you call the deal.'

His strong jawline hardened. 'I don't see a problem or a conflict of interests. You get to wear fabulous clothes, live in a superb apartment and enjoy the high life for a couple of months.'

'I can see that you believe that that should be a big draw, but it's not.' Lifting her head with determined composure, Misty walked to the door.

'What more did you expect?'

'Respect…for a start.' Misty pushed out that admission between gritted teeth.

'That has to be earned…and I doubt your ability to earn mine.'

Did having bad luck in business make her so much a lesser person? Did he only respect successful people with big bank balances and social pedigrees? He really was obnoxious. He had had no need to make that last comment. It suggested a prejudice against her that both shook and mortified her, for he might have enquired into the state of her catering business but surely he could know very little else about her?

'I shouldn't have said that. I'm sorry,' Leone Andracchi drawled flatly.

'Don't let it worry you,' Misty advised, registering that he was merely concerned that he might have overplayed his hand and not truly regretful. 'You're self-satisfied, arrogant, manipulative and ruthless. You could have given me that contract, for I believe you're well aware that I would've worked my socks off to fulfil it. However, you prefer to use my problems as a weapon against me. You have very little conscience and even less compassion. Do you really think I'm surprised that you should also be very rude?'

And with that concluding accolade Misty skimmed him a flashing glance from her silver grey eyes. He was very still. Pretty much gobsmacked by that retaliation. Hard dark eyes assailed hers in a seering look that was pure naked intimidation.

'I shouldn't have said that. I'm so sorry,' Misty told him with an insincerity that more than equalled his own a minute earlier, and with that she left his office at speed.

Hit and run? Was that all she was good for? She had been scared that he might have a temper the size of his powerful personality. But biting the hand that she might end up having to feed from was real insanity. Right this very minute, he would be comforting himself with that superior awareness and thinking how stupid she had been to risk alienating him to that extent. And it was surely paranoiac of her to believe that he might have deliberately withheld that contract to put her under more pressure to agree?

In fact it was most likely that he had turned to her because some other woman had refused. A fake mistress? Why? What was Leone Andracchi up to? Such an extraordinary proposition *and* an expensive one if he was planning to put her in some fancy apartment and furnish her with an appropriate wardrobe. So somehow it would have to profit him. But as she went down in the lift, still shell-shocked by their interview, she could not work out how setting up a pretend mistress could possibly benefit him.

She pictured that lean dark face, breathtakingly good-looking, devastatingly cool and unrevealing. Nobody would ever accuse of Leone Andracchi of wearing his thoughts on his sleeve. A shiver of foreboding ran down her spine. As she crossed the spacious foyer on the ground floor her steps slowed. What was she doing walking away from his rescue bid?

In return for her playing some ridiculous role as his mistress, he would save her business and enable her to continue paying the mortgage on Birdie's home as well as ensure the ongoing employment of her staff. When the rewards were so great and so many other people would suffer if her business failed, what was a couple of months out of her life? What had been the point of walking out on Leone Andracchi when in reality she had no choice but to accept his terms? She had no other options, had she?

Misty had to make herself walk back into the lift; the prospect of eating humble pie had no appeal. In the short corridor which led to Leone's office on the top floor, she was disconcerted to see him standing outside the door in conversation with two men. She came to an awkward halt a good ten feet away, two high spots of pink forming over her cheekbones. It took her just two seconds to decide that he was deliberately ignoring her, a lowering impression only increased by the sight of him looking so infuriatingly at ease. Arrogant dark head held at an angle, his jacket pushed back by the lean hand he had thrust in the pocket of his tailored trousers, he emanated relaxation. Angry resentment stiffened her to stone.

Finally, Leone turned his head and lifted an enquiring ebony brow, lean strong face urbane.

'The answer's…*yes*,' Misty framed with flat emphasis.

His brilliant dark eyes gleamed and he stretched out a hand. In the very act of turning away to make good her escape while he was occupied, for she really had had enough of him for one afternoon, Misty stilled. With frozen reluctance, she moved forward, horribly conscious of his companions' curiosity as they stepped back out of her path.

His wide sensual mouth curved into a slow, charismatic smile that made her mouth run dry. He caught her fingers in his and closed an arm round her.

'Excuse me…' he murmured huskily to their audience, pressing open the door of his office to back her over the threshold.

'What on—?' earth are you playing at, Misty began to say.

Warning dark golden eyes assailed hers and before she could utter one more syllable he had whirled her round and brought his mouth crashing down on hers with devouring sexual hunger. An inarticulate moan of shock was dragged from her but, in the split second in which she was incredulously aware that the wretched door wasn't even closed to conceal them, his passionate intensity scorched her into sensual awakening. As he banded his hands round the curve of her hips and pressed her into intimate connection with every muscular line of his big, powerful body, raw excitement flamed through her quivering length like a forest fire licking out of control.

His tongue plundered the moist, tender interior of her mouth in a devastatingly erotic invasion, every explicit probe of that lancing exploration driving her sensation-starved body crazy. Her heart hammering, she was fighting for oxygen but clinging to him, conscious of the unmistakable thrust of his arousal, inflamed rather than repelled by that evidence of his masculine hunger.

A febrile line of colour accentuating his superb cheekbones, Leone released her and snatched in a ragged breath. 'I think that was an impressive enough statement of our intentions.'

Less quick to recover, Misty pulled in a lungful of air like a drowning swimmer, her legs feeling barely strong enough to support her as she instinctively fell back against the wall for support. She couldn't credit what had just happened between them. It wasn't just that he had grabbed and kissed her; it was the infinitely more disturbing truth that she had revelled like a wanton in that passionate embrace. She was shattered by the betrayal of her own body, the response that he had demanded and extracted without her volition.

'Our intentions?' Misty framed unevenly, noting that the corridor was now empty, face burning at the appalling awareness that she, who prided herself on behaving in a professional manner in a business environment, had just committed the ultimate unforgivable sin.

'Too good an opportunity to miss,' Leone quipped, slumbrous dark eyes veiled by his lush black lashes.

She was so enraged by that explanation that she wanted to slap him into the middle of the next week. 'You *said* that you weren't into sexually harassing employees.'

'If you think that we're likely to convince anyone that we're intimately involved without an occasional demonstration of lover-like enthusiasm, you must be very naive,' Leone countered drily. 'But it will only be for public consumption. In private the act dies.'

'You don't need to tell me that.' Not trusting her temper

in his vicinity and bitterly conscious that she had burnt her boats without taking the time to consider the potential costs of such a role, Misty compressed her lips hard. 'May I leave now?'

Leone flicked her a considering glance. 'Yes. I'll see you at my hotel tonight at nine and we'll get the remaining details ironed out. I'm staying at the Belstone House hotel—'

'Tonight doesn't suit me,' Misty said facetiously, unable to resist the temptation.

'*Make* it suit,' he advised. 'I'm returning to London tomorrow.'

With a rigid little nod of grudging agreement, Misty walked back out again, her slender spine ramrod straight. But she was even more angry with herself than she was with him. How could she have lost herself like that in his arms? But then she had never felt like that before with a man, no, not even with Philip in the first fine flush of love. She paled, suppressing that unfortunate thought. What she had felt at nineteen was hard to recall three years on. Leone Andracchi had caught her off guard. Self-evidently, he possessed great technique in the kissing department, but why hadn't her loathing for the man triumphed?

Colouring and confused by what she could not explain to her own satisfaction, Misty climbed into the van in Brewsters' car park and drove to the premises she rented on the outskirts of town. There she joined her three staff in the clean-up operation that concluded every working day. It was after five by the time she locked up and all she could think about was how her business had become so vulnerable that one lost contract could finish it off.

Carlton Catering was just over a year old. She had started out small, doing private dinner parties and the occasional wedding. Nothing too fancy, nothing too big and her overheads had been low. But when, five months ago,

her supplier had mentioned that there was a tender coming
out for providing lunches at Brewsters, the biggest, swank-
iest company on the industrial estate, she had been eager
to put in a bid and expand. On the strength of that trial
contract, she had borrowed to buy another van and upgrade
her equipment.

However, disaster had struck soon afterwards. Her
premises had been vandalised and the damage had been
extensive but her insurance company had refused to pay
out, arguing that her security precautions had been inade-
quate. That had been a bitter and unexpected blow, for the
repairs had wiped out her cash reserve and from that point
on she had been struggling to stay afloat.

'Your need to reduce your personal expenditure to offset
that loss,' her bank manager had warned her only six
weeks earlier. 'In spite of your cash-flow problems, you're
continuing to pay the mortgage on a house that doesn't
belong to you. I respect your generosity towards Mrs
Pearce, but you *must* be realistic about the extent of the
drain on your own resources.'

But sometimes being realistic utterly failed to take account of circumstances and emotional ties like love and
loyalty, Misty reflected painfully as she drove home.
Birdie Pearce lived in a rambling old country house called
Fossetts, which had belonged to her late husband Robin's
family for generations. Unable to have children of their
own, Robin and Birdie had chosen to become foster parents instead. For over thirty years the kindly couple had
opened their home and devoted their lives to helping
countless difficult and disturbed children.

Misty had been one of those foster kids and she too had
been unhappy, bitter and distrustful when she had first
gone to Fossetts. She had been twelve years old, hiding
behind a tough front of not caring where she lived or who
looked after her, but Birdie and Robin had worked hard to

gain her trust and affection. They had transformed her life
by giving her security and having faith in her, and that was
a debt she knew that she could never repay but, above all,
it was a *loving* debt, not a burden.

For the past fourteen months, a fair proportion of
Misty's earnings had gone towards ensuring that Birdie
could remain in her own home. Not that Birdie knew that
even yet, for her husband had once managed their finances
and Misty had taken over that task after the older man's
death. Misty had been shocked to discover that Fossetts
was mortgaged to the hilt. When Robin's investments had
failed and money had become tight, he had borrowed on
the house without mentioning the matter to anyone.

Now over seventy, Birdie had a bad heart and she was
on the waiting list for the surgery that would hopefully
ensure that she lived well into old age. But in the short
term, without that surgery, Birdie was very vulnerable and
her consultant had emphasised how important it was that
Birdie should enjoy a stress-free existence. Birdie loved
her home and it was also her last link with Robin, whom
she had adored. From the outset, Misty's objective had
been to protect the older woman from the financial worry
that might bring on another heart attack. But even Misty
had not appreciated just how much it would cost to keep
Fossetts running for Birdie's sake.

It was a tall, rather Gothic house with a steep pitched
roof and quaint attic windows. Built in the nineteen twen-
ties, it sat in a grove of stately beech trees fronted by a
rough meadow. Parking the van, Misty suppressed a troubled sigh. Fossetts was beginning to look neglected. The
grounds no longer rejoiced in a gardener. The windows
needed to be replaced and the walls were crying out for
fresh paint. Although it was far from being a mansion, it
was still too big a house to be maintained on a shoestring.

Yet the minute Misty stepped into the wood-panelled

front hall, she felt for a moment as though all the troubles of the day had slipped from her shoulders. On a worn side table an arrangement of overblown roses filled the air with their sweet scent and dropped their petals. She walked down to the kitchen, which was original to the house and furnished with built-in pine dressers and a big white china sink.

Nancy was making salad sandwiches for tea. A plump woman in her late fifties, Nancy was a cousin of Robin's, who had come to live at Fossetts and help out with the children almost twenty years earlier. These days, she looked after Birdie.

'Birdie's in the summer house,' Nancy said cheerfully. 'We're going to have tea outside.'

Misty managed to smile. 'Sounds lovely. Can I help?'

'No. Go and keep Birdie company.'

It was a beautiful warm June evening but Birdie was wrapped in a blanket, for she felt the cold no matter how good the weather. She was a tiny woman, only four feet eleven inches tall and very slight in build. Her weathered face was embellished by a pair of still-lively blue eyes. 'Isn't the garden beautiful?' she sighed appreciatively.

Misty surveyed the dappled shade cast by the trees, the lush green grass of early summer and the soft pink fading show of the rhododendron blooms. It was indeed a tranquil scene. 'How have you been today?'

Birdie, who hated talking about her health, ignored the question. 'I had visitors. The new vicar and his wife. They've hardly been living here five minutes and already they've heard those silly rumours about how I've been reduced to genteel poverty by some greedy former foster child.' Birdie tilted her greying head to one side, bright eyes exasperated. 'Such nonsense and so I pointed out. Where on earth are these stories coming from?'

'That business with Dawn, I expect. Someone's heard

something about that and got the wrong end of the stick.'
Misty neglected to add that the more curious of the locals
had evidently noted the visible decline in the Pearce for-
tunes and put the worst possible interpretation on it. But
then over the years that the Pearces had fostered, more
than one pessimistic neighbour had forecast that they
would live to regret taking on such 'bad' children.

And sadly, the previous year, Dawn, who *had* once been
fostered by the Pearces, had come to visit and had stolen
all Birdie's jewellery. Birdie had refused to prosecute because Dawn had been a drug addict in a pitiful state. Since
then, yielding to Birdie's persuasions and her own longing
to reclaim her life, Dawn had completed a successful re-
habilitation programme but none of the jewellery had been
recovered.

'Why do people always want to think the worst?' Birdie
looked genuinely pained for she herself always liked to
think the very best of others.

'No, they don't,' Misty soothed.

'Well, what have you got to tell me today about that
handsome Sicilian at Brewsters? I would love to get a peek
at a genuine business tycoon. I've never seen one except
on television,' Birdie said naively, for all the world as
though Leone Andracchi were on a level with a rare animal.

Misty smiled at the little woman, but a great surge of
loving tenderness made her eyes prickle and she had to
look away. She told herself that she ought to be copying
Birdie's sunny optimism, turning her problems round until
a silver lining appeared in the clouds. And, lo and behold,
Leone Andracchi began looking more like their saviour!
So why the heck was she still festering with anguished
loathing over one stupid kiss? Was she turning into an
appalling prude?

'Actually...Mr Andracchi's offered me work in London.'

Misty's gaze was veiled, for she could not have looked Birdie in the eye and told that partial truth. 'How would you feel about me going away for a month or two?'

'To work for a handsome millionaire? Ecstatic!' Birdie teased after she had recovered from her surprise at that sudden announcement.

After tea, Misty went upstairs and opened the wardrobe which contained the clothing that Flash had insisted on buying her in an effort to lift her out of her depression after Philip had broken off their engagement. Fancy frivolous designer garments that had not seen the light of day in over two years. She selected a turquoise *faux* snakeskin skirt and top and a pair of spiky-heeled shoes. After a quick bath, she dug out her cosmetics, which dated from the same period and which had been similiarly shelved after she had said goodbye to her brief foray into Flash's glitzy, unreal world.

Flash had transformed her into a rock-star chick and she had learned how to make the best of her looks. Not that it had been much comfort then to see a sexy, daring image in the mirror when the man that she had loved had rejected her. It had wrecked things between her and Flash too, she acknowledged with pained regret. The day Flash had made her fanciable on his own terms had seemed to be the beginning of the end of their friendship. He had stopped thinking of her as a sister, stopped seeing her as the skinny little kid who had shared the same foster home with him for almost five years and had decided that he wanted more.

Making use of the elderly car that only Nancy used now, Misty drove over to the country house hotel where Leone Andracchi was staying. The gracious foyer exuded expensive exclusivity, and when she enquired at the desk she was informed that Leone was in the dining room.

While she hovered, working out whether she ought to wait or seek him out in the midst of his meal, a fair-haired male emerged from the lounge bar and stopped dead at the sight of her, reacting in a similiar vein to the doorman, who had surged to open the door for her, and the male receptionist, who had tripped over a waste-paper basket in his haste to attend to her.

'Misty…?'

For a split second, Misty thought she was dreaming for, even though it had been three years since she had heard it, she recognised that hesitant, well-bred voice immediately and she spun round in shock. *'Philip?'*

'It's been so long since I've seen you.' Philip Redding stared at her; indeed, his inability to stop staring was marked. 'How a-are you?' he stammered.

'Fine…' Her lips barely moved as her silver-grey eyes lingered on him for, although they still lived within miles of each other, she had been careful to avoid places where they had been likely to meet and, apart from seeing his car on the road occasionally, had been very successful in ensuring that they had not run into each other again.

'You look…you look quite incredible.' His colour heightened as he found himself forced to tilt his head back to meet her gaze. 'I've often thought of calling in at Fossetts—'

'With your wife and children?' Misty enquired in brittle disbelief.

Philip paled and stiffened. 'Just the one child…Helen and I are getting a divorce, actually…it didn't work out.'

Twenty feet away, Leone Andracchi stilled, stunned by the vision of Misty Carlton shorn of her shapeless grey suit. With her wealth of copper hair tumbling loose, eyes that gleamed like polished silver were soft on the face of the man she was regarding, her wide peach tinted mouth parted to show pearly teeth. Leone could not quite work out what she was wearing. The top seemed to be held up by the narrow chains bisecting her slight shoulders. The rich fabric gleamed beneath the lights accentuating the thrust of her breasts, the slender indent of her waist, and screeched to a death-defying halt above long, long, endless legs capable of stopping traffic.

'Misty…?'

Taken aback by Philip's blunt admission that his marriage was heading for the divorce courts, Misty shifted her attention to the tall dark male poised several feet away. Leone Andracchi. She collided with sizzling golden eyes that seemed to burn up all the available oxygen in the atmosphere and instantly she tensed, butterflies fluttering in her tummy. But even as she reacted to his vibrant presence her mind was marching on to make uneasy comparisons between the two men. Leone was much taller, more powerfully built and strikingly dark next to Philip with his boyish fair good looks.

'Sorry if I've kept you waiting, *amore*,' Leone murmured smooth as silk, moving to her side to place an infuriatingly possessive hand on her spine.

'Philip Redding…' Philip shot out a hand with all the easy friendliness that was natural to him. 'Misty and I are old friends.'

'How fascinating,' Leone drawled in a tone of crushing boredom that made the younger man flush. 'Unfortunately, Misty and I are running late.'

'Look, I'll call you,' Philip told Misty, giving Leone a bewildered look, quite out of his depth when faced with such a complete lack of answering courtesy.

'Don't waste your time,' Leone advised before Misty could respond, shooting Philip a derisive glance of cold menace as he pressed her over to the lift and hit the call button with one stab of a punitive finger. 'She won't be available.'

Her face flaming but her lips sealed, for she could not intervene when she did not *want* Philip to phone Fossetts and upset Birdie, Misty stalked into the lift while listening to Philip mutter in disconcerted response, 'Well, I must say…really, for goodness' sake…'

'Do you like behaving like the playground bully?' Misty enquired dulcetly as the lift doors whirred shut.

'While you're with me, you don't talk to other men…you don't even *look* at other men,' Leone delivered with simmering emphasis.

Misty clashed head-on with brilliant golden eyes that went straight for the jugular and a bone-deep charge of grateful excitement surged through her long, slender length for the very last thing she wanted to think about just then was Philip, whose rejection had torn her apart with grief and despair for longer than she cared to recall. 'Is that a fact?'

'Particularly old flames…' Leone decreed, impervious to sarcasm.

Misty tilted her copper head back and shrugged a slim shoulder, glorious silver eyes wide and mocking, the knot of sexual tension he had already awakened licking through her like a dangerous drug in her bloodstream. 'Then you had better watch me well.'

'No. I'm paying for total fidelity and the illusion that you have eyes for no other man,' Leone imparted without hesitation. 'Flirting with Redding was out of line.'

'Flirting…?' An involuntary laugh empty of humour was wrenched from Misty, the emotions roused by that unfortunate encounter with her ex-fiancé breaking loose of her control. 'Philip's the last man alive I'd flirt with!'

'I saw the way you looked at him,' Leone said with grim clarity.

'And how was that?' Misty queried unevenly, curious in spite of herself.

'Do I need to draw pictures?'

Her silver-grey eyes darkened as a shard of bitter pain

from the past assailed her but she veiled her gaze in self-protection. So for an instant she had recalled happier times when Philip had meant the world to her, but those days were very far behind her. And why was she so sure of that reality? Three years earlier, she had only been engaged to Philip for six weeks when a drunk driver had crashed into Philip's car. Although Philip had sustained only a concussion, Misty had suffered internal injuries and had required surgery. Afterwards she had learned that she might never be able to conceive a child and Philip had found the threat of a childless future impossible to accept. But never let it be said that Philip was unfeeling: after all, he had had tears in his eyes when he'd ditched her, when he'd told her that he'd still loved her but that she wasn't really a *proper* woman any more...

'Redding was all over you like a rash—'

'He didn't even touch me!'

'He didn't get the chance.'

As Leone rested a lean hand on Misty's spine to prompt her out of the lift again, she jerked away and flung her bright head high, sending him a warning look from bright silver eyes. 'I don't see an audience, so keep your hands to yourself!'

CHAPTER THREE

MISTY'S eyes leapt in skittish mode round the luxurious hotel suite while she struggled to disguise the fact that her whole body wanted to shake as if she were a leaf in a high wind.

She could not credit that that brief meeting with Philip should have brought so many wounding memories to the surface and destabilised her to such an extent. But then she had worked long and hard to bury all that pain, to rise above the cruel concept that fertility was the sole measure of femininity, and had learned to focus on another future other than that of a husband and a family.

'Would you like a drink?' Leone Andracchi enquired.

'No, thanks.'

'Possibly it might calm your nerves—'

Misty whirled round in a surge of fury that erupted so suddenly it made her feel dizzy with the strength of it. 'There's nothing wrong with my nerves! Stop trying to put me down—'

Brilliant dark golden eyes rested on her. 'So the wimp upset you—'

'Don't talk about Philip like that...you don't know him.'

'I don't need to,' Leone purred, surveying her with sardonic amusement. 'He showed himself up.'

Misty threw back her head, copper hair flying back from her flushed cheekbones. 'No, I think *you* did. I don't like aggressive men.'

A slow, winging smile slanted his wide, sensual mouth. She had the maddening suspicion that, far from her draw-

42

ing blood with her retaliation, he was actually enjoying the exchange. 'I'm not aggressive…I'm strong and you like that.'

'I don't know what you're talking about.'

A winged ebony brow quirked. 'Don't you?'

She could feel the tense silence buzzing around her. Her mouth had run dry and her heart was thumping like a trapped bird against her ribs. She looked at him: so very tall and lean with the sleek, honed, muscular build and grace of a natural athlete. His cropped, slightly curly black hair gleamed in the lamp light that picked out every fabulous angle of his bone structure, accentuating the carved cheekbones, the hollows beneath, the firm, sensual line of his mouth. Drop-dead gorgeous, as she had been refusing to acknowledge from the moment he'd appeared in the downstairs foyer and shadowed Philip like Everest looming over a bump in the lawn.

Entrapped by those smouldering dark golden eyes, she could look nowhere else and every breath that quivered through her felt like a huge effort. The taut peaks of her breasts ached and a sliding, curling sensation low in her pelvis made her tighten her thighs. Her knees had developed a slight tremor and all the time she was aware only of the almost terrifying rise of anticipation that took account of nothing but the fierce longing gripping her.

'You want me…I want you, but it's not going to happen,' Leone breathed in a charged undertone that rasped down her sensitive spine like a roughened caress. 'This is strictly business and we don't need to make it complicated.'

Stark disconcertion rippled through Misty. She felt stripped naked, exposed. Urgent words of proud denial brimmed on her lips until she saw the way his burning gaze was homed in on her mouth and she trembled, the excitement climbing again, mindless and without conscience.

'Business…' Leone repeated thickly.

Someone rapped on the door and, although the knock was light, Misty flinched, dredged from her fever with a sense of guilty embarrassment. As the door opened and a young man appeared with a file in his hand she turned to stare out the window, breathing in slow and deep, fighting to still the nervous tremors currenting through her. Nobody had ever had so powerful an effect on her and it was starting to scare her: it was as if she had no control over herself around him, as if her brain went walkabout. But *he* was feeling that pull too. That shook her, surprised her, made her feel a little less mortified. Although she knew that the worst thing she could do would be to lower her guard around a male like Leone Andracchi, the knowledge that the attraction was mutual still made her feel better about herself, better than she had felt in a long time.

The door snapped shut and she turned back.

'This is the agreement I mentioned.' Leone extended a document. 'Read it and then sign.'

Misty accepted the document. 'And if I don't sign?'

'We don't have a deal.'

She sat down and began to read. It was typical employment contract stuff, no mention of her pretending to be his mistress or of clothes or apartments either. However, there was a clause that said she would forfeit all benefits and payments if she tried to walk out before he considered the job complete. She didn't like, that but her attention was caught by the sum of cash he was offering in return and that amount bereft her of breath. Enough money to keep the mortgage on Fossetts ticking over for the next year and more, as well as allowing sufficient funds to settle her outstanding bills and cover staff salaries during her absence.

Cheeks burning, Misty swallowed hard and looked up. 'You're being very generous…but what am I supposed to think about this bit that says I can't walk out on this without your agreement?'

'You may think what you like,' Leone murmured levelly, 'but I assure you that the position won't entail anything either immoral, illegal or dangerous.'

None the wiser, but still troubled that he saw the necessity of making that stipulation, Misty lifted the pen from the table in front of her. He wasn't going to explain himself and she couldn't afford to throw away the only lifebelt on offer.

'Wait…' Striding back to the door, Leone called the young man back in to witness her signature and his own.

Such devotion to legal detail rather unnerved Misty. When the document was duly removed, she smoothed her damp palms down over her skirt. 'Now what?'

'Just a few details. I'll send a car to pick you up at nine on Monday—'

'This Monday coming?' Misty questioned. 'That's only six days from now—'

'I want this show up and running for the following weekend.' Leone settled a notepad down on the coffeetable. 'Make a note of your measurements. You need a new wardrobe.'

Misty bridled at both the instruction and that announcement. 'I already have quite a few presentable outfits—'

'But maybe I'm not into the rock-chick look.' Leone dealt her startled face a sardonic appraisal. 'Maybe I prefer a more elegant and subtle image.'

Rock chick? Misty coloured with annoyance and chagrin, for her top only bared her arms and her skirt was not that short. However, she was more concerned by what his choice of that particular label had revealed. 'You know about Flash, don't you? How?'

'Don't be so naive. Do you really think I would've offered you this role without knowing anything about you?'

When he put it like that, he did make her sound naive, but she didn't like the idea that he had run some sort of a check on her background. He had contrived to make a connection known to precious few and, after her time with Flash, Misty had soon learned that just about everybody who *did* know assumed that she had slept with her former foster brother and that arguing otherwise made little impression.

'There's nothing wrong with what I'm wearing,' Misty said defensively.

Leone surveyed her with exasperated dark golden eyes. 'Tell me, is it your special mission in life to argue with my every simple request?'

'You don't request, you *order*, but bearing in mind that this is supposed to be a job, I'll try to be more receptive.'

'Thank you *so* much.'

Misty drew in a deep steadying breath. Tight-lipped, she filled in her measurements on the notepad, tossed it aside and said equally drily, 'Anything else?'

'Have you always found it this difficult to follow instructions?'

Misty nodded in grudging acknowledgement.

Leone shifted a fluid and expressive hand. 'It's very irritating.'

Misty folded her arms with a jerk. 'Anything else happening next Monday?'

'You get a complete make-over and move into the apartment. We'll go out in the evening—'

'Where?'

'I haven't decided yet. Any questions?'

None that Misty thought that he would answer, and she stood up. 'Is that it, then?'

'I'll see you out to your car—'

'No need,' Misty said in surprise.

Leone swung open the door for her exit and said nothing.

Teeth gritting, Misty stood in the lift with him in silence.

Head high, she crossed the foyer and stalked out onto the steps where a lean hand caught hold of hers.

'What?' Misty snapped, forced to swing back.

Leone closed her other hand into his too. She connected with smouldering golden eyes that sent her heartbeat racing and her tummy gave an apprehensive somersault. 'Don't…'

Black lashes low over his slumbrous gaze, Leone stared down at her with vibrant amusement. 'Stop trying to pretend it's a punishment, *amore.*'

Her colour heightened and her slender body quivered as he drew her closer. His sensual mouth drifted down onto hers with an aching sweetness that took her wholly by surprise. She trembled and almost without her own volition pressed forward into the hard, muscular heat of him, every skincell in her body leaping in excited reaction. It was an intoxicating kiss—searching, erotic, teasing, and she could not get enough of that sensual exploration. A low moan sounded deep in her throat.

Leone set her back from him. 'A very convincing pretence,' he murmured with roughened satisfaction.

Her fingers jerked in the grip of his, her anger provoked by an intense sense of embarrassment. 'You—!'

'Temper, temper.' A wry smile slashed his lean, strong face.

Misty dragged her hands free of his and said icily, 'Goodnight.'

Halfway across the car park, she glanced over her shoulder and saw that he had moved to the foot of the steps to watch her progress. Not quite as confident in dark car parks as she liked to pretend, Misty was relieved. She was digging into her bag for her keys when a male figure appeared from behind Birdie's car and a gasp of fright broke from her lips.

'It's only me, Misty,' Philip groaned. 'I recognised Birdie's old car and parked behind it—'

'You scared the life out of me!' Misty settled her bag on the bonnet of the car to better enable her search for her keys, furious that she hadn't got them out before leaving the hotel and rigid with discomfiture in Philip's radius.

'I'm sorry, but I thought it would be easier to talk to you here rather than at Fossetts where I'm sure I'm not very popular—'

'We don't have anything to talk about. I'm sorry that your marriage has run into trouble…*genuinely* sorry,' Misty stressed awkwardly without looking at him. 'But it's not as though we're even friends any more, is it?'

'Just listen to me. I never got over you,' Philip swore emotively. 'I was crazy to rush off and marry Helen—'

'I don't want to hear that kind of stuff from you.' Keys in her shaking hand, Misty struggled to find the lock and make good her escape. 'Please go home.'

'You heard her. Back off.' It was Leone, his dark, deep, accented drawl as welcome at that moment as a rescue squad, his shadow blocking out Philip's, his long, sure fingers removing the keys from hers to unlock the door of the car. In her surprise and relief, she glanced up at him, noting how the aggression he had earlier denied was stamped into every line of his lean, powerful face, but not one atom of that aggression was aimed at her. Philip was the unhappy recipient and Philip, she saw out of the corner of her eye, had already backed off so far that he would need a loud hailer to continue their dialogue.

'Thanks,' Misty said raggedly, diving into Birdie's ancient car at supersonic speed.

'No problem. Did that idiot scare you?' Leone demanded.

'No…' Misty lied, attention nervously lodged to the clenched fist within view. 'No, not at all.'

Without another glance at either man, she drove off, but she stopped a mile down the road to wipe her tear-wet face dry with a tissue. No, she no longer cared about Philip, but her memories hurt terribly. How could Philip even think that his interest might still be welcome after the way he had treated her?

Within six months of ditching her, he had married a well-bred blonde with a cut-glass accent and a double-barrelled surname—exactly the sort of young woman his snobbish mother had always wanted him to marry. And within a year he had become father to a beautiful baby boy. Misty might not have seen Philip in recent years but she *had* seen his wife and child out shopping on several occasions. She would never forget the pain of first seeing their baby and knowing that that special joy was unlikely ever to be hers. It seemed all wrong too that the son that Philip had sworn he could not live without having some day should now be caught up in the miseries of a divorce.

Sucking in a steadying breath, Misty drove home. After she had got over Philip, she had forced herself out on dates purely to please Birdie. But when she had casually encouraged those men to share their aspirations, she had discovered that they too took it for granted that their future would hold children and paled at the gills at the mere mention of a woman with fertility problems.

It was one thing for a man to marry a woman unaware that there might be a problem in that department, another thing entirely for him to do so armed with that knowledge. That took either a very special love or a male who didn't want kids. So to protect herself from that horrible sinking feeling of inadequacy, of seeing herself as something less than other women and of having to ultimately face confiding the consequences of that car smash in any more lasting relationship, she had given up on dating and had concentrated on setting up her business instead.

And she had been perfectly happy and content until Leone Andracchi had come along and reminded her that she was still a woman and still susceptible to all the feelings and fancies that she had foolishly assumed she could shut out and ignore. In his vicinity she had all the resistance of a schoolgirl with a bad crush and that hammered her pride hard. But what worried her most was the awareness that Leone Andracchi fascinated her: his every move fascinated her, even though he infuriated her.

Had he insisted on seeing her out to the car park because he'd suspected that Philip might still have been hanging around? Or had that just been coincidence? Surely it must have been coincidence. Yet why was she receiving the impression that, even when Leone was faking a caring role, he was a very possessive guy with the women in his life? After all, he seemed prone to standing over her like a Rottweiler guarding a bone!

But obviously she had picked up the wrong impression and Leone was simply a good actor, for Clarice had brought in a couple of glossy gossip magazines in which he had featured with various beauties and Misty had formed a picture of a very different male. A guy so cool in relationships that ice might be cosy in comparison. A guy who got bored very easily and without apology, generous to a fault but ungiven to commitment or romantic gestures, indeed the guy most likely to forget your birthday, overlook St Valentine's Day and cancel dates last minute in favour of work. A guy whose lovers always looked nervous, as if at any moment they awaited the news that they were no longer flavour of the month. In short, an absolute rat, whom any sensible woman would avoid like the plague…as would she to the best of her ability.

On the day that Leone had arranged, Misty arrived in London. While the chauffeur removed her two bulging suitcases from the boot of the opulent limousine that had collected her from Fossetts, Misty stared up at the massive ultra-modern apartment building shadowing the pavement.

Over the last week, while she had closed up her business premises and made a dozen last minute arrangements to take care of various matters, she had been conscious of a positively childish little glow of growing excitement. She was embarrassed by that reality but had been forced to concede that her life had been pretty uneventful for a long while. Although she would hate seeing less of Birdie, the change of scene was especially welcome after the stress and worry she had suffered in recent months.

Travelling up in the lift, she studied her reflection in the mirrored wall and frowned. All anxious eyes and mouth, she thought ruefully, no alteration there, nothing very special either, although Leone must have seen something to have behaved as he had. Unfortunately, her self-esteem had sunk to an all-time low after Philip and had never really recovered. After all, that self-esteem had been a hard-won achievement even *before* Philip had entered her life.

So many people had broken promises to Misty that it had taken a very long time for her to learn to trust anyone. She could still recall her mother clear as day: a beautiful redhead with lovely clothes and a constant embattled air of uneasy apology.

'As soon as I get organised, you can come and live with me,' her mother had promised repeatedly when Misty had been living in care. 'I gave your sister up for adoption…you know she was sickly and I could never have managed her…but I couldn't bring myself to give you up as well.'

But Misty had lived from birth to adulthood in foster care and by the time she was five her mother's occasional visits had become only a memory. Years later, it had been a shock to discover that her parent had remarried within eighteen months of her birth and that there had never been any question of her bringing her illegitimate daughter into the marital home when her second husband was not even aware of Misty's existence.

A trim older man in a steward's jacket introduced himself as Alfredo at the door of the apartment. She stepped into a very large hall floored in marble and glanced into a reception room, which rejoiced in minimal modern furniture and a decor of white on white. The only colour she could see came from the artworks on display. It was fashionable and elegant but cold and unappealing, she reflected in some disappointment.

Well, what had she expected? she asked herself ruefully. Cosy clutter? Having shown her into a spacious bedroom complete with dressing room and *en suite* facilities, Alfredo passed her a sheet of paper headed, 'Appointments.' At that point, Misty realised that a busy afternoon lay ahead of her at various beauty establishments and she grimaced. Evidently, Leone was of the opinion that in the looks department she needed all the professional help she could get!

By the end of those appointments some hours later, her hair coaxed into a streaming mane and her practical short nails disguised by fake perfection, Misty had decided that being a mistress, pretend or otherwise, promised to be the most boring existence imaginable.

The limousine was on the way back to the apartment and stuck in the teatime traffic when Leone called her on the car phone. 'I'll pick you up at seven,' he informed her, the rich timbre of his dark, deep drawl making her spine tingle.

She breathed in deep. 'Where are we going?'

'A movie première.'

'Oh…' Misty was disconcerted, not having expected anything like such a grand public occasion.

'Wear the jewellery,' he told her huskily. 'I chose diamonds for you.'

Back at the apartment she went straight to her bedroom. A shallow heart-shaped case sat on the dressing table and she clicked it open to a breathtaking diamond necklace and drop earrings. Dragging her attention from them in astonishment, she noted that her suitcases had disappeared. An examination of the dressing room not only revealed that her luggage had been unpacked but also revealed a large selection of new garments in her size. In addition, a long slinky silvery gown with slender straps hung in apparent readiness for her and it carried the label of one of the world's most exclusive designers.

At half-past seven, Misty strolled into the vast lounge where Leone was poised by the floor-deep windows. Even from the back he looked spectacular: sunlight gleaming on his proud dark head, wide shoulders tapering to narrow hips and long, powerful legs.

'I don't like being kept waiting,' Leone delivered before he even turned round.

'You didn't give me much warning.' Misty stilled, copper head high, slim body taut as she waited for him to look at her.

He swung round. '*Dio mio*…you spent the entire afternoon getting ready!'

Dark golden eyes glinting with impatience zeroed in on her and then narrowed to stare.

Misty knew that she had never looked better. The shimmer of the silver and the glitter of the diamonds flattered her copper hair and fair complexion and the dress was a dream of deceptive simplicity cut to enhance her slender curves. A fashionable frilled split ran to high above her knee and revealed one slim, shapely leg shod in a kitten-heeled diamanté shoe.

The silence was electric.

'You look fantastic,' Leone breathed in another voice entirely, his rich drawl roughening. His screened gaze roamed from her silvery eyes and the glow in her triangular face to linger on the ripe pout of her burgundy tinted mouth before travelling on downward to absorb the full effect of the dress.

Beneath that intent scrutiny Misty's mouth had run dry and she was alarmingly short of breath. Aware of his vibrant masculinity with every skincell in her thrumming body, she fought to get a grip on a sudden inexplicable sense of euphoria. 'Thank you.'

'That doesn't mean that you're forgiven for keeping me waiting,' Leone asserted in the hall.

'You might as well get used to it,' Misty dared. 'Outside business hours, I'm always running late—'

'This *is* business,' Leone reminded her drily.

As he stood back for her to enter the lift colour lit her taut cheekbones. 'Then don't look at me the way you do.'

'Looking's not touching,' Leone murmured, smooth as silk.

Her teeth ground together. He had, it seemed, an answer for *everything*. She climbed into the limousine with frustration currenting through her. The whole time she had been getting dressed, she had marvelled at the lengths to which he was willing to go to establish their masquerade. The apartment, the clothes, the fabulous jewellery, not to mention the cost of winning her agreement—it had all come at a high price. What could he hope to achieve from such a pretence? Her imagination had run riot. She had even wondered if he was having an affair with a married woman and attempting to establish a mistress as a cover story.

'I wish that you would tell me what this is all about,' she said tightly. 'I swear that I would keep it quiet.'

Leone stretched his long, powerful length into an indolent attitude of relaxation. He surveyed her from below dense ebony lashes. 'By the time this finishes, you will no longer be in the dark as to my motivation.'

Something in his voice sent a shiver down Misty's spine. 'I don't think I like the sound of that.'

'I'm paying you well for your services,' Leone countered with crushing cool.

Her temper sparked. 'Courtesy costs nothing,'

'You're too proud for your own good.' Leone rested measuring eyes on her, lean dark features impassive.

Misty stared back at him, her facial bones tight. 'I feel like a doll you've dressed up!'

'Worry if I start trying to *un*dress you,' Leone advised in a jungle-cat purr.

She couldn't help it: her face flamed and, although she had been dying to ask what the film was, she said nothing for the remainder of the drive.

Even before they emerged from the limo, she saw the press cameras and the crash barriers holding back the crowds waiting to see celebrities arrive. Her nervous tension started to rise. Cool as ice, Leone walked her between the barriers with a light arm at her spine. She was quite unprepared for the sudden question shouted by a journalist.

'Who's the new lady, Leone?'

And without the smallest warning, the cameras were turned on them along with a whole new barrage of questions, which Leone ignored. A smile stuck to her numb mouth like paint, perspiration dewing her short upper lip, Misty was intimidated by the surge of interest and the photos being taken. What on earth would Birdie think if she opened a newspaper and saw Misty, who had supposedly come to London to *work*, attending a film première with diamonds hanging from her ears? How was she to explain that development? Why the heck hadn't it occurred to her before now that a male who made regular appearances in the gossip columns was likely to attract that kind of media attention?

'You should've warned me it would be like this,' Misty muttered minutes later, her low-pitched voice full of reproach. 'I had no idea that my being with you was going to be such a public event.'

Leone dealt her a sardonic appraisal. 'Ditch the artless routine. Why do you think you're looking so good? Only married men hide their mistresses.'

'Well, I can tell you right now that being *your* mistress stinks!' Misty hissed furiously out of the corner of her mouth.

'If we were playing this for real, you wouldn't be talking like that,' Leone drawled in purring provocation, his breath fanning her cheek, and she coloured furiously as she caught an older woman watching them and realised how intimate his pose must seem.

Before the lights went down, Misty engaged in looking out for famous faces and spotted several. Her self-consciousness only returned when she realised that she was under examination too by several sets of curious eyes. The film was an edge-of-the-seat thriller and she thoroughly enjoyed it. Before the credits were rolling down the screen, Leone whisked her out again. Emerging into the brightly lit street, she froze at the sight of the waiting cameras.

'Ignore them and smile,' Leone murmured as he felt her stiffen in discomfiture.

As the limo door closed on them he flashed her a look of exasperation. 'Why the shrinking-violet act?'

'I don't want my photo in the newspapers!' Misty protested. 'I don't like people talking about me!'

'You...*don't*?' Leone queried in a tone of mockery.

The silence buzzed.

Leone leant forward, extracted a DVD from a storage unit and fed it into the player below the built in television. He zapped the control and lounged back in the corner. 'I just want to remind myself of how shy you are in public...'

Misty frowned in bewilderment as the television screen came to life to show Flash on stage at one of his concerts, and then a split second later her heart sank as she realised *which* concert it was. There she was dancing like a wanton show-off, hair everywhere, wild-eyed, skimpy little dress showing far too much thigh. She broke out in nervous perspiration. Her fingers knotted, nails scoring welts into her palms. Her lowest moment...and somehow *he* had discovered that that ghastly performance of hers had been captured for posterity on film, which was more than she had known herself. In all her life, she did not believe she had ever felt more humiliated or embarrassed than she did at that instant.

'Switch it off!' Misty pleaded in a desperate rush.

'I'm looking hard for signs of timidity,' Leone confided. 'There you are in front of thousands of people—'

'*Please* switch it off!' Misty gritted feverishly.

'Don't be so selfish,' Leone scolded her with a slow, mocking smile that made her face burn even hotter with squirming chagrin. 'The camera loves you and I'm sure the guys in the audience loved you too. You're very sexy.'

Misty made a wild grab at the remote he held in one lean hand, but he stretched it out of reach. 'If you don't give me that control, I'll-'

'You'll...what?' Leone prompted with amusement.

'You don't understand...Flash *dared* me! I'd been drinking, I didn't care about anything that night...'

Registering that she was telling him things he had no right
to know and merely increasing her own mortification, and
recognising that the cynical glint in his dark golden eyes
had merely heightened, Misty lost what remained of her
hold on her temper and threw herself at him to retrieve the
control.

'*Accidenti!*' Leone exclaimed, finding himself engaged
in a physical struggle with something of his bemusement
showing in his lean, strong face. 'Are you crazy?'

'Give it to me!' Misty raked at him, straining over him
to stretch a hand up to his.

'When I pictured you on my lap,' Leone savoured with
roughened intensity as he dropped the remote and closed
both lean hands round her slender forearms at speed, 'this
isn't quite the way it was, *amore.*'

Infuriated at the position he had trapped her in, Misty
snapped, 'Let *go* of me!'

Instead he drew her fully down on him. Smouldering
dark golden eyes lodged on her startled face. 'You should
think twice before you climb on top of a guy and ask him
to give it to you…'

Belatedly she realised that her dress had ridden up and
that the most sensitive part of her whole body was pressed
to the hard, surging masculine arousal of his. Her breath
caught in her throat, heat flaring through her in an accel-
erated surge of sexual awareness. 'You know I didn't
mean—'

'And right now,' Leone murmured with mesmeric hus-
kiness, his brilliant eyes holding hers as he anchored one
hand into the fall of her copper hair to ease her forward.
'I am very tempted to satisfy your request.'

He locked his hot mouth to the tiny pulse flickering like
crazy below her collar-bone and a shudder of response
hotter than any fire raked through her. Her head tipped
back, one hand grabbing at his shoulder to steady herself,

a strangled little moan torn from her throat. Her breasts were taut and full, her nipples straining. He bent her back over one strong arm and let his sensual mouth rove over her exposed cleavage, driving her mad with frustrated longing for more. Shock was leaping through her in waves for her own hunger had surged so fast in response to his that she was breathless and her heart was beating so fast she was afraid it would burst.

'*Dio…*' Leone growled, gathering her up in his arms and laying her down full length on the smooth cream leather seat. 'I don't want to stop…'

CHAPTER FOUR

MISTY clashed with Leone's burning golden eyes and just lay there, every inch of her drawn tight with screaming anticipation.

He hit a button and the flickering lights of the city streets showing through the tinted windows were screened out, locking them into greater privacy. He shed his jacket in a fluid but purposeful movement. He plucked off her shoes, cast them aside and then he reached for her again.

'I...' she began, nervous second thoughts prompting her at the exact same moment as Leone's carnal lips locked to hers with urgent hunger.

It was like going to heaven on a rocket. The explosion of passion jolted her. His tongue plundered the tender interior of her mouth, setting up a chain reaction through her quivering body. He slid a hand beneath her hip, lifting her to him, and she locked her arms round his neck, letting that wild kiss deepen to the brink of cutting off her own oxygen supply.

With a harsh rush of breath, Leone lifted his dark head, colour scoring his superb cheekbones, golden eyes shimmering over her. Unclasping her hands, he drew the straps of her dress down over her arms. 'I want to rip that dress off you and the silk would tear like paper, but we *do* have to vacate the car at some stage,' he pointed out with audible regret.

Shock shrilled through her as he unzipped her dress and cooler air hit her exposed flesh. She was breathing in rapid, irregular little gasps, striving not to think of what he had just said, but her brain had begun to turn again. They were in a car. Did she want to lose her virginity on the back seat of a car? All right, so it was a limo, but right now his chauffeur probably had a very good idea of what his passengers were doing and she would have to walk out past the man and pretend she didn't mind him thinking she was a real little…a real little slut…

'You have gorgeous breasts…' Appreciative golden eyes scorched over the pert, pouting mounds now bared for his appraisal.

In thrall to the conviction that she was behaving like a wanton, she glanced down at her own nakedness and almost had a heart attack. But her immediate effort to cover herself with her hands was thwarted by the simple fact that he was holding them.

'In fact, I don't think a brief sortie is likely to satisfy me.' Leone lowered his head to run the tip of his tongue over a quivering pink nipple and her spine arched in an involuntary spasm of response, an ache stirring with powerful effect between her thighs.

'No…?' she gasped, too controlled by tormenting sensation to catch her breath.

He closed his mouth round a lush rosy peak and caught her sensitive flesh between his teeth in a teasing, sensual assault. She could not restrain the low, keening cry that escaped her parted lips. A knot of unbearable tension was tightening low in her pelvis. She wanted him, she wanted him as she had never wanted any male. Somewhere in the background she was dimly conscious of the faint sound of music, familiar music that tugged at her memory. Then Leone let his fingers tug at her distended nipples and thought was snatched from her again with a vengeance. Excitement had her in its tenacious hold. She was lost in the fierce hunger of her own body

'I'm going to screw you senseless, *amore*,' Leone intoned with raw sensual force, sinking his hands beneath her hips to tug her dress out of his path. 'And then I'm going to take you into my bed tonight and do it all over again.'

A combination of shock, excitement and shame hit her all at once. But even as that threat excited her to an embarrassing degree the words jarred on her: too raw, too realistic. And in the background she finally recognised the melodic sound of the song that Flash had written for her and inwardly cringed at her own weakness with Leone Andracchi. How could she have been so stupid as to allow matters to get so far? Leone would just be using her for sex. He didn't care about her, he didn't even *like* her, for goodness' sake! That she found him sheer, tormenting temptation was no excuse. And letting him have her on the back seat of his limo would be the ultimate in tarty behaviour. Surely she had more respect for herself?

'What's wrong?'

It shook Misty that he had noted her withdrawal that fast. She snaked back from him and sat up in an awkward movement, frantically wrenching at her dress in an effort to yank it up and cover her breasts at speed. There was a ghastly ripping sound that made her squeeze her stinging eyes shut in despair. But the electric silence that stretched was even tougher on her nerves.

'You've changed your mind,' Leone breathed not quite steadily.

'I'm sorry,' she mumbled shakily. 'I wish I'd changed it sooner but this…*us*…well, it's a really bad idea. As you said yourself, strictly business is wiser.'

'You want me to make a deal that includes access to your body as well?' Leone derided in a tone that stung her sensitive nerves like a whiplash.

In a sudden motion, she turned round and hit him so hard with her open palm that a shuddering sensation ran up her arm and her hand went numb. 'Don't you dare talk to me like that! I'm not some whore available for a price!'

A silence that left the previous silence behind in the starting stakes had fallen. A perfect imprint of her finger-tips was burned into the olive skin above his aggressive jawline and his golden eyes were molten with outrage and shock.

'I'm not going to apologise for hitting you either,' Misty framed on the back of an overwrought sob. 'It's a pity someone didn't thump the hell out of you a long time ago! Just because you're not used to a woman saying no.'

'I didn't argue. I freed you immediately,' Leone grated in a ferocious undertone. 'There is no excuse for you striking me when you know that I can't hit back.'

Misty was trembling. She sat up, dragging at the dress until it stretched back over her breasts. She was scared to look to see where the delicate silk had torn. She dived into the shoulder straps and began to struggle to do up the zip.

'Let me,' Leone said icily, turning her round to run up the zip with the merest touch, as though he were risking radioactive contamination.

'Thanks.'

He sent the blinds flying back from the windows with the stab of one lean finger. She wanted to open the passenger door beside her and throw herself out even though the limo was still moving. His wounding words had bitten deep and sent her careening into the kind of loss of control she had not surrendered to since childhood, and in the aftermath she was in shock and ashamed but she couldn't bring herself to apologise for slapping him after what he had said.

The limousine drew up. The chauffeur opened the passenger door. As she sat there, frozen with knowledge that her once-beautiful gown was now ripped right up to her waist, something warm and heavy was draped round her shoulders: his jacket. She drew in a quivering breath and began to climb out. An arm curved round her, keeping the jacket in place, Leone walked her into the well-lit foyer and exchanged a word with the unctuous doorman, who went to call the lift for them.

Inside the lift the silence was so profound that it buzzed in her ears. She couldn't bring herself to look at him until it occurred to her to wonder why he was accompanying her. Just to get his jacket back? She glanced up. His lean, powerful face was set in forbidding lines, stunning eyes veiled and dark.

He used a key on the apartment door and tossed it on a side table. She slid out of his jacket and extended it.

He hooked it with one lean brown hand. 'Goodnight,' he said without any expression at all.

As he strode in the direction of the bedroom corridor, Misty cleared her throat. 'Where are you going?'

'To have a long cold shower,' Leone framed in a gritty tone. 'You have a problem with that too?'

Her face flamed. 'I meant...you're staying the night *here*?'

'I don't sleepwalk,' Leone assured her very drily.

Finally she added two and two and made four for herself. Her full mouth compressed. 'You're staying because I'm supposed to be your mistress. So I'm a put-out-on-the-first-date girl now as well as everything else...'

'I beg your pardon?' Leone had swung back.

Misty surveyed him with silver-grey eyes awash with resentment. He was a visual joy and she was questioning now if her susceptibility to those stunning dark good looks of his had dulled her wits a week earlier. She had not foreseen the costs she would pay in terms of her own reputation, but she *should* have done. In a small business like hers, the reputation of a female owner was all important. Nobody was ever likely to take her seriously again after she had been seen draped round Leone Andracchi wearing diamonds and designer garments. That was bimbo territory. The few who had accepted that Flash was just a very good friend would now suspect otherwise. People would decide she was a gold-digging tart who threw herself at any rich man who came within her reach and female clients would be none too keen to hire her services.

'You heard me.' She folded her arms with a jerk. 'If you stay tonight, you're making me look like a tramp.'

'I'm so grateful that you're *not* my mistress.' Thrusting lean brown fingers through his tousled black hair, Leone surveyed her with an aura of sardonic satisfaction. 'You saved us both from making a serious error of judgement this evening. Feel free to hit me any time I get too close in the future.'

Anger stiffened her. 'I really am starting to *hate* you—'

'Hold the feeling, nourish it,' Leone advised with silken mockery. 'Because if you ever end up in bed with me, life as you know it will end.'

Misty flung her head back, lustrous copper coils of hair falling back from her slanted cheekbones, grey eyes silver with rage. 'Oh yeah?'

A wolfish grin of appreciation slashed his lean dark features. For a split second all the charisma he had bent over backwards to conceal from her flashed out full force and she found herself staring, hooked like a fish on a line. 'Oh, *yeah*,' he emphasised huskily. 'I'll be gone before you get up tomorrow. I'll see you Friday. We're heading up to Scotland for the weekend.'

And with that concluding assurance he strolled with fluid grace down the corridor, leaving her standing there like a woman who had just seen exactly what she did not want to see. A male genuinely capable of fascinating her, a male who could shift within the space of minutes from icy reserve to sardonic humour to that self-mocking smile, which had made her stupid heart sing and bang like a drum.

Snatching in a ragged breath, Misty walked down to her own room, closed the door and leant back against it for a moment, feeling oddly empty. She lay awake in the moonlight and was shaken to discover her mind wandering to an imaginary vision of Leone having a cold shower. Feeling the heat of a self-loathing blush, she rolled over and stuffed her face in a pillow. She relived her own wild, wanton craving for him in the limo and squirmed with discomfiture.

When she had heard other women talking about not being able to resist some guy, she had never been too impressed. After all, she had not even found Philip irresistible. In her teens, she had had to come to terms with the cautionary tale of her own mother's mistakes and deep down inside, although she had never admitted it even to Birdie, she had been afraid that she might turn out to be the same as her mother, Carrie, who had mistaken lust for love. Carrie had flitted from one relationship to the next and left a trail of destruction and abandoned children in her wake.

Misty had been studying at catering college when she'd met Philip. From that first week, they had been inseparable and he had seemed so romantic and caring that she could never, ever have guessed what the future had held for them both.

Right from the start, however, Philip's mother had been cold with Misty, and one afternoon the older woman had said with revealing distaste, 'You really don't know what's in your background, do you?'

And, sadly, that had been true for it said 'father unknown' on Misty's birth certificate. She was illegitimate and had no relatives to offer even on the maternal side. Philip had had to stand firm against his mother's efforts to break them up and Misty had believed that he'd truly had to love her to have withstood that pressure. Once they had become engaged, Misty had begun feeling more secure in their relationship and, although until that point she had always called an anxious halt to their lovemaking, she had finally agreed to go away for the weekend with him. A dream weekend in a historic country hotel. But they had never arrived: on the way there, they had had the car accident and that had been that as far as she and Philip had been concerned.

After falling into an uneasy dose, Misty wakened soon after dawn feeling thirsty. Rolling out of bed, she freshened up in the *en suite* and, having tugged on her wrap over her nightie, she padded out into the corridor to go in search of the kitchen. As she walked past the dining room, she almost cannoned into Alfredo, who was carrying a coffee pot.

'Misty?' It was Leone's dark drawl.

Misty hovered awkwardly in the doorway. He looked gorgeous. Having risen from the breakfast table in courteous acknowledgement of her appearance, immaculate in a grey business suit worn with a snazzy dull gold tie, Leone shifted an inviting hand. 'Join me.'

Slowly she shook her copper head in wonderment.

'Why are you staring at me?' Leone asked.

'You're such a contradiction. I walk into the room and you stand up. Someone taught you very good manners—'

'My mother,' Leone slotted in drily.

'But it was such a waste of time when you can hardly open your mouth around me without being offensive.' Misty sighed, settling down into a seat opposite and reaching for the jug of orange juice.

Disconcerted, Leone breathed in deep, brilliant dark golden eyes shimmering as he sank back down again. In the electric silence, broken only by the manservant's reappearance, Misty poured herself a glass of pure orange and sipped. Alfredo poured Leone's coffee and, grey eyes dancing with amusement, Misty sugared it for him with a teasing hand.

'So where are you off to at this early hour?' she asked brightly as she pounced on a warm croissant and began to eat it.

'Paris…'

'I was there once but I didn't really see it. I was with Flash. Either we were in the hotel hiding from his horde of screaming fans or I was backstage.'

Leone's intent scrutiny was lodged on her lush pink lips as the tip of her tongue snaked out to retrieve a stray crumb. As she noted the path of his attention, a slow burning curl of heat ignited in her pelvis and she shifted on her seat. Cold shower time, she thought guiltily, horribly conscious of her own vulnerability. In a frantic attempt to distract herself, she focused on the portrait on the wall. She had noted it the day before. It was the sole piece of traditional art she had so far seen in the apartment: an oil of a young girl with a dreamy expression in her dark eyes.

'That's a lovely painting,' she remarked brittly. 'Anyone you know?'

Right before her eyes, Leone froze, lean, strong face clenching hard. 'My sister…she's dead.'

Misty paled, lips parting and then sealing again before she made a desperate effort at recovery. 'Well, at least you had her for a while.'

His forbidding frown would have silenced a lesser woman. 'And what's that supposed to mean?'

Misty sucked in a steadying breath and wished that she had stuck to muttering conventional regrets. 'I…er…well, I have a twin sister that—'

Fortunately that sudden announcement seemed to grab his attention. 'You *know* that you have a twin?'

'We're not identical…that's about all I do know about her.' Misty shrugged, regretting having raised so personal a subject yet grateful that they had moved on from the too sensitive topic of his own sister's death. 'She was adopted and I wasn't.'

'One would've assumed that twins would have been kept together,' Leone remarked with veiled eyes.

'When it came to my sister and I, our mother was willing to sign away her rights to her but not to me as well. I tried to establish contact with my twin through the private adoption agency when I was a teenager but she wasn't interested. I just got a letter back saying that her adoptive parents were all the family she needed and that she didn't want to meet me. Birdie thinks that she may change her mind when she's older.' Misty forced an accepting smile, as if that negative response hadn't been any big deal, but the fierce disappointment and hurt of that rejection still lingered. She had had such high hopes and those hopes had been shattered by that chilly little letter bare of even an address lest she make a nuisance of herself by arriving on the doorstep.

'Birdie…your foster mother,' Leone answered for himself.

'You know a lot about me.' Before she had slept the night before, Misty had mulled over that little scene in his limo and his cruelly manipulative playing of that recording of Flash's concert in Germany. 'I think you could've been more up front about that.'

'I was *very* up front on that score last night. You struck me,' Leone reminded her.

Misty reddened to the roots of her hair. 'All right, I shouldn't have done that but you provoked me!'

Stunning dark golden eyes nailed to her with relentless force, Leone lounged back in his chair. 'That's not an excuse.'

'I lost my temper.'

'Try again.'

Misty could feel that forbidden anger mushrooming all over again. 'I'm sorry…I'm *sorry*…I'm sorry…OK?' she reeled off on a rising note.

'Who says you can't take a horse to water and *make* it drink?' Leone murmured with cool satisfaction.

Misty drew in a deep shaken breath and counted steadily to ten.

'I have to leave.' Tossing down his napkin, Leone rose to his full intimidating height. He strode away and then paused and wheeled back round again, lean, strong face taut. 'If anyone contacts you or visits you during my absence, you tell them absolutely nothing about our relationship and you stay in role. Agreed?'

Disconcerted, Misty nodded slowly. Was he expecting someone to call on her?

As he strode out into the hall she leapt off her chair and hurried in pursuit, determined to ask the question that had niggled at her the evening before. 'Leone…?'

His screened gaze ran from the crown of her tousled copper head, down over her simple white nightshirt and wrap and the long, slender legs beneath, before running back up to rest on her pink cheeks. 'Did anyone ever tell you that you look luscious at six in the morning?'

'Do you ever think of anything but the obvious around a woman?' Misty asked ruefully.

'Did no one ever teach you how to receive a compliment?' Leone demanded.

'Look, I have this question I want to ask…' She linked her hands together. 'Are you having an affair with a married woman and trying to set me up as your cover story?'

'I don't have affairs with married women. Sharing a woman would never come naturally to me.'

She reddened but continued, 'So this *is* a business thing—'

'Sicilian business,' Leone qualified, smooth as black velvet. 'You wouldn't understand the nuances.'

'I suppose not...' Misty watched him depart.

After he'd gone, she read the newspapers over breakfast and her heart sank to her toes. A recognisable picture of her on Leone's arm featured in two different gossip columns. 'Leone's latest squeeze,' she was called in one and 'Another Andracchi beauty' in the other, which she knew that Birdie read every day. So far she had not been identified but how long was that happy state of affairs likely to last? After that wretched kiss Leone had stolen at Brewsters, local gossip would have got a headstart even before she'd headed for London. She realised that she had been really stupid to believe that she could get away with telling Birdie that she was *working* for Leone. Appreciating that she had to explain herself, she caught the train back to Norfolk and a cab ferried her out to Fossetts from the station.

By then, it was mid-afternoon and Birdie was in the sitting room fixing flowers at a table by the window. She looked up with a tranquil smile, only the faintest hint of concern in her bright eyes. 'I suppose you left *him* in London.'

'Birdie...I—'

'You're in the throes of a big romance and you didn't tell me,' Birdie scolded. 'But why are you looking so worried? I'm happy that you've met someone that you can care about again.'

Misty worried at her full lower lip with her teeth, not knowing how best to respond.

'Obviously you've moved *in* with him, as they call it these days,' Birdie continued ruefully. 'I don't approve of that aspect, but I do understand why you couldn't bring yourself to tell me.'

'I'm sorry.'

'You're a dear girl,' the older woman murmured with quiet affection. 'And if Leone Andracchi hurts you, he'll have me to reckon with.'

The ridiculous image of tiny Birdie calling Leone to account made Misty smile and she murmured gently, 'Stop fretting about me.'

'I expect Flash will now tell you that his heart is broken and he'll write a song about it. You had better brace yourself. There's nothing that young man loves more than a challenge…except perhaps an audience.'

Misty stayed on at Fossetts for a couple of days and took the train back to London on the Thursday afternoon, feeling pleasantly rested. When Alfredo opened the apartment door to her that evening, he was wearing a rather hunted expression.

'I really must have a key of my own,' she said gently.

'So that you can come and go as you please?' A familiar dark drawl launched from the lounge doorway. 'Not in this lifetime!'

Misty came to a dead halt in the centre of the hall. Leone was poised only fifteen feet from her. A green cotton shirt pushed up his muscular brown forearms, fitting black jeans sheathing his lean hips and long, powerful thighs, his sheer exotic appeal was only outweighed by the scorching anger glittering in his hard golden eyes.

'What's the matter?' she asked hesitantly, totally thrown by that greeting.

Leone spread both arms in a very expansive gesture. 'You are asking *me* what's wrong? Within hours of my flight to Paris, you walked out of here and vanished into thin air!'

'I've been at home with Birdie.'

'Not according to her housekeeper. I phoned and asked for you.'

Misty winced. Having identified her as being the woman with Leone at the première, a local journalist had repeatedly phoned asking to be put in contact with her. Mercifully having fielded his first call for herself, Misty had asked Nancy just to pretend that she wasn't there if there were any further enquiries in that line, and there had been several from different sources.

'So where *have* you been? Because if you've been with Philip Redding, I'm going to rip him apart!'

Misty surveyed him in growing wonderment.

'I should have dealt with him in the car park that night,' Leone framed with unconcealed aggression.

'Do you think you own me…or something?'

The silence sizzled.

'For the next few weeks…*yes*.' Smouldering golden eyes challenged her. 'If I find out that you've been screwing some other guy…'

Misty folded her arms and surveyed him with furious resentment and chagrin. 'You really do think I sleep around, don't you?'

'No…comment.'

'I was at Fossetts with Birdie keeping a low profile—'

'So *low* nobody knew you were there,' Leone slotted in unimpressed. 'Do you think that I can't recognise an alibi when I hear one?'

'Women do this to you all the time, then…do they?' Misty widened big grey eyes in mock sympathy. 'Sneak off to have it away with other men—'

'*Per meraviglia!* No woman has *ever* done that to me!' Leone sent her a flashing look of outraged denial. 'And don't stray off the subject. Were you with your ex-fiancé?'

'No…but to be honest, I don't think I'd tell you if I had been,' Misty confided. 'You didn't ask me not to leave

London. You said you'd see me on Friday and it wasn't Friday last time I looked at the calendar. As far as I was concerned, I was off duty.'

Leone was still endeavouring to swallow her first statement and it appeared to be a major challenge. 'You wouldn't tell me if you *had* been with Redding?'

'As I wasn't, it's a moot point.' Misty yielded a little for the sake of peace.

'Were you *on* or *off* duty in my limo the other night?'

Her face burned. 'What do you think?'

With a sudden frown of exasperation, Leone glanced at his watch. 'I'm running extremely late for a dinner date. I'll see you tomorrow afternoon. We're flying up to Aberdeen and driving the rest of the way.'

Like a woman turned to stone by that careless speech, Misty watched Leone depart. He had a date. He... had...a...*date*. And he wasn't returning to the apartment either, so no prizes for guessing how *he* planned to while away the night hours. But then what did his sex life have to do with her? She had no idea, but she still couldn't settle at anything for what remained of the evening and she was dismayed to find her thoughts continually turning to what Leone might be doing. Obviously his current lover was either a very understanding woman or in on the secret that he refused to trust his fake mistress with. It was a job, just a job, and when had she forgotten that? When she had been writhing on the back seat of his limo? Hating herself for that degrading memory, she went to bed and swore that from then on she would not forget for one second that she was simply his employee.

The following day, she was taken to the airport to meet Leone. A paparazzo was standing by with a camera to mark the occasion and Leone greeted her with an embrace. Convinced that the photographer's presence was no accident and resenting that reality, Misty twisted her head away to ensure that Leone's kiss landed on her cheek instead.

'Why did you do that?' Leone demanded.

'Kissing's very personal…a hug is just as convincing,' Misty told him stonily.

'Really? I just hugged a block of wood.'

Matters were not helped by the four-hour delay on their flight, which followed as the result of an air traffic controllers' strike. In the VIP lounge, Leone worked at his laptop while she leafed through various magazines. Every time she looked at him, he annoyed her. He looked so sophisticated and handsome in his designer country casuals and a svelte blonde on the other side of the room kept on throwing him flirtatious glances, evidently having decided that Misty was merely an adjunct. And she wasn't important, was she? In fact, she was just nobody in Leone Andracchi's life. But last night, he had been with a somebody who *was*…

'Are you planning to defrost before we arrive with our hosts?' Leone enquired on the walk out to his private jet.

'I haven't a clue what you're talking about. I'm here, I'm all dressed up and I'm smiling. What more do you want?'

'You didn't sugar my coffee…it was quite deliberate and unbelievably childish,' Leone derided.

'You can fetch your own coffee from now on. I'm not your little *slave*,' Misty hissed like a spitting cat.

Not a word was shared during the flight, not even while the jet endlessly circled above the airport awaiting a landing slot. By the time they climbed into the car awaiting their use, after she had watched Leone attempt without success to call their hosts to explain why they would be so late, it was almost seven and their weekend trip was showing all the promise of a developing nightmare in which everything that could go wrong did go wrong.

'*Dio mio!* Why is no one answering the phone?' Leone growled. 'It's a castle…the Garrisons must have a large staff.'

'You mean, you haven't visited these people before?' Misty was quick to take the opportunity to satisfy her curiosity without losing face. A castle? Now that sounded interesting to her.

'Never. I hardly know the Garrisons but I believe they're quite elderly.'

Leone said that he knew where he was going even though he had never been there before and refused the offer of the tiny map inside the tourist brochure that she had picked up to amuse herself with at the airport. She fell asleep and at some timeless stage later was quite briskly shaken awake.

'We're arrived,' Leone said darkly.

'Where?'

'The end of the bloody world,' Leone growled with a distinct lack of appreciation.

CHAPTER FIVE

MISTY clambered out of the car, shivered in the surprisingly cool air and rubbed her hands over her bare arms before reaching for her jacket. All she could see beyond the car was a towering building with not a single light in sight. 'What time is it?'

'Ten.'

As Leone thumped at the massive front door knocker, Misty resisted an urge to ask if he had taken the scenic route to the castle. 'Did you manage to phone the Garrisons while I was asleep?'

'No.' After waiting two minutes, Leone hammered the knocker with greater vigour.

Several more tense minutes passed and then finally a dim light glowed into life above them and they heard a heavy bolt being drawn back. Leone looked only marginally less grim.

An old man wearing a wool dressing gown peered out at them. 'Are you wanting to wake the whole castle up? Have you no idea what time it is? It's after *ten*…'

Misty hid a smile under her hair while Leone, impervious to that censorious complaint, introduced himself, banded an impatient arm round her back and urged her over the threshold. A dying fire was flickering in the giant grate of the big hall, casting long shadows on panelled walls the colour of dark honey and the worn flagged floor.

'Oh, this is lovely…' Misty sighed.

'I'll show you to your room, then,' the old man grumbled.

'And you are?' Leone prompted in quiet command.

'Murdo, sir…'

'We'd like to offer our apologies for our late arrival to your employers,' Leone continued.

'You'll not be doing that tonight. They're in their beds.' Murdo led the way to the winding stone staircase in the corner of the hall. 'We only keep late hours at Castle Eyrie on special occasions.'

After a lengthy hike down gloomy corridors lit with very low-wattage bulbs, the old man opened the door of a bedroom. 'If you're wanting anything to eat, you'll have to see to yourselves. The kitchen's off the long corridor at the back of the hall.'

Watching Leone's lean dark features radiate disbelief at the offering of that helpful information, Misty hurried to offer an admiring comment about the bedroom which earned her a grateful smile from the lugubrious Murdo.

Only after the older man had gone did Misty wrench her appreciative gaze from the charming curtained oak four-poster bed and the carved wooden chimney-piece to contemplate the reality that they had only been shown to *one* room. Why hadn't that likelihood occurred to her before? And there was nowhere to sleep apart from the bed.

'*Per meraviglia*…it's freezing in here! It's probably damp.' An incredulous look of hauteur on his lean strong face, Leone glanced into the adjoining bathroom and barely concealed a shudder at the sight of the ancient fixtures. 'There's not even a shower!'

'There's only one bed…'

The bathroom doorknob came off in Leone's hand and he thrust it back on again. 'The whole castle is in an advanced state of decay. No wonder the Garrisons have the place on the market! I expect some romantic fool and his money will soon be parted.'

'There's only one bed…'

'Yes…as there are only three pieces of furniture in the

entire room, I *had* noticed that,' Leone derided. 'But right now, I'm rather more interested in heat and food.'

'You could light a fire and I'll make us something to eat.'

'This is not quite what I expected from a weekend in the country—'

'Will you stop complaining?' Misty gave him a look of reproach. 'It's obvious that the Garrisons are struggling to survive and can't afford more home comforts or staff.'

'You couldn't be more wrong. They're rich and stingy and famous for underpaying their workers. Their fortune was made in garment manufacturing sweatshops abroad,' Leone informed her drily. 'Save your compassion for more deserving parties.'

In spite of the kitchen being a giant cellar-like space that did not appear to have been updated since the Middle Ages, the fridge was large and well-stocked and in no time at all, blithely ignoring Leone's comments about the amount of logs it took to fill the grate in their bedroom, she had Spanish omelettes and a bowl of Caesar salad sitting on the old pine table. They both ate with appetite and little need for conversation.

Back upstairs again with the flickering fire casting a wonderfully atmospheric and flattering glow over the worn furnishings, Misty stole an embarrassed glance at Leone. 'I really *wasn't* expecting to have to share a bed with you.'

'Do you think our hosts, the Garrisons, actually still exist?' Leone mused, gazing down reflectively into the fire before he turned his dark head, vibrant dark golden eyes assailing hers with heart-stopping amusement. 'Or do you think old Murdo has done away with them and we're the next on the list? Do you want me to sit up all night armed with a poker?'

No, I want *you*, Misty thought in shaken acknowledgement of the jealous feelings of possessiveness and hurt that had been tormenting her since the night before. *I want you in that bed with me.* So stark was the voice telling her that inside her head that for an awful moment she actually feared that she had spoken those words out loud. Dragging her self-conscious gaze from him, she turned away. 'I'm going for a bath. I'll be quick.'

Gathering up her things from the case she had yet to unpack, she backed over the threshold in haste and then she paused, suddenly deciding to throw caution to the four winds and just satisfy herself. 'Who were you with last night?'

'With friends I hadn't seen in some time.' Leone studied her with veiled eyes that now betrayed a glitter of infuriating awareness. 'So *that* is what wound you up overnight.'

Feverish pink flooding her cheekbones, Misty closed the door in haste. Although on one level she wished she had had the self-discipline not to ask that leading question, on another she was too relieved by the answer she had received to care beyond the cringing knowledge that she had embarrassed herself. She soon discovered that the water was barely lukewarm and there was no temptation to linger.

'There's no hot water,' she said, returning to the bedroom shivering in the fancy silk nightdress that was all she had bothered to pack and striving to pretend it was nothing out of the ordinary for her to be sharing a bedroom with a man.

Already halfway out of his shirt, Leone rested measuring dark golden eyes on her hectically flushed face in the light cast by the flickering fire. 'Do I need to drench myself in cold water again tonight?'

The silence simmered.

Misty had not expected a question that direct. Dredging her shaken scrutiny from his bronzed muscular chest and the tangle of dark curls sprinkling his pectorals, she scrambled into the bed at speed. 'Yes,' she said tightly.

There would be no giving way to temptation, she told herself urgently, and she refused to look at him while she mustered her defences. Their current intimacy was deceptive. It wasn't real and it meant nothing. She fancied him like mad, had never known that desire could bite so deep, but her sane mind warned her that at best she would only be a temporary distraction for Leone Andracchi. Their only true relationship was an unusual working agreement and if those boundaries were breached it would get messy, embarrassing and far too personal. Indeed, she would just be asking to get a kick in the teeth.

Finding that her teeth were chattering, she sat up and finally noticed that the window was wide open, letting in a brisk breeze. In exasperation she leapt out of bed and hurried over to close it. No sooner did the fire get going than he opened a window! Where was the sense in that? She soon found out as smoke began to billow out of the grate and she was forced to throw the offending window wide open again.

The bathroom door opened. She hunched up under the covers but lifted her lashes a half-inch to see Leone emerge wearing only a pair of boxer shorts. She shut her eyes again but he was etched in her memory in glorious Technicolor: black hair still damp above his lean, chiselled features, wide, smooth brown shoulders, superb torso, sleek hips, long, hair-roughened thighs. Stop it, stop it, *stop* it, she urged herself guiltily.

The mattress gave under Leone's weight and then there was a ripping sound and he loosed a curse and vaulted back up again. As the covers were flipped back from her, she was forced to sit up and contemplate the long tear in the threadbare bottom sheet. 'How the hell am I supposed to sleep on top of that?' Leone demanded.

'I can fix it.' Misty was eager to be doing something and she got up.

'We should go to a hotel—'

'We'll manage fine.' Yanking off the bedding, Misty removed the bottom sheet and turned it so that the rip would lie below the pillows. 'Come on…help me!'

'It's a disgrace to treat guests like this,' Leone ground out.

'But it's such a wonderful old building, full of history and atmosphere *and*—'

'Damp and discomfort?'

As Misty straightened from tucking in the bedding again, something caught at her hair and out of the corner of her eye she saw a large moth and she yelped. 'Is it still in my hair?'

'It won't do you any harm.' With infuriating cool, Leone shooed the moth out into the night again.

Misty rested back against the foot of the bed, pale and struggling to catch her breath again. Leone studied her with shimmering golden eyes. The very awareness she had been seeking to avoid with too much chatter and an attack of practical housekeeping ripped through her taut length in a fiery charge.

'Standing there in the firelight you might well as be naked,' Leone breathed thickly.

Glancing down at herself in dismay, noting the way the flames shone through the delicate silk, she groaned and made a sudden move to dive back into bed. But before she could get there Leone reached for her and hauled her into his powerful arms.

As his hungry mouth came crashing down on hers, a startled squawk was silenced in her throat. Excitement hurtled up inside her like a lightning strike. Suddenly, without any warning or any sense that her brain was prompting her, she was winding her arms round him and clinging.

His fingers splayed across her hips, urging her into connection with the straining thrust of his erection, sending a sharp arrow of primitive need arrowing up from her pelvis, an instinctive reaction that had nothing to do with thought but everything to do with the stormy passion he had ignited.

He lifted her up onto the bed and tumbled her across it, following her down, kneeing apart her thighs with a confident domination that not a skincell in her quivering body wanted to resist. He was kissing her with a hard, deep urgency that was setting her on fire. She could not get enough of his mouth. Every so often she drew back to draw in an agonised gasp of oxygen and then went back for more, her hands curved to his well-shaped head, fingers sliding and curling through the damp black strands as she held him to her.

Finally Leone lifted his head, his own breathing harsh and uneven, brilliant golden eyes bright below ink-dark lashes. 'Are you protected?'

A shard of unwelcome reality pierced her brain. Protected? Protected from pregnancy, her thoughts completed. Oh, yes, she was protected all right, she thought with sudden bitter pain, protected by her own virtual inability to conceive. 'Yes...'

The tension holding Leone's big, powerful body taut over hers ebbed and he gazed down at her with burning satisfaction. 'This was inevitable, *amore*.'

'Was it?' While her intelligence prompted her to think about what she was doing, her entire being was a seething, seductive mass of response. The scent and the touch of him, the very weight of him against her thigh were a potent aphrodisiac. She could not bring herself to break free of him.

'The minute I saw you, I wanted you.' Leone reclaimed her reddened lips in a probing and erotic assault that was pure intoxication. 'The sun was coming through the window and your hair was like a halo of fire…'

Her eyes fluttered wide on his lean, strong face, heart racing as she checked out that he had actually said that. He screened his gaze, hard jawline clenching, faint colour scoring his incredible cheekbones as if he wasn't any more used to saying that sort of thing than she was used to hearing it. 'Sexy…'

The strangest shard of tenderness tugged at her as he ended with that rather lame but much cooler conclusion. And then he kissed her again and the world spun as if she were on a roller coaster, heart thumping, body braced in the teeth of the wind.

'I can't get enough of you,' Misty muttered in a daze.

Leone gave her a slow-burning smile, relocated them against the pillows and buried his hot mouth against her aching breasts, palming the small mounds through the fine silk, making her spine arch and her breath catch in her throat. 'I can be addictive… I should have warned you, *amore.*'

She closed her eyes while he took off her nightdress.

'*Dio mio*…you're perfect,' Leone growled, catching a distended pink nipple between thumb and forefinger and sending a spasm of tormented reaction through her, strong enough to make her moan.

Her eyes opened on the leaping shadows of light and dark that marked his darkly handsome features and she discovered that he was staring down at her with a slight frown. 'What?'

'You're lying there as if you are *so* shy,' Leone confided with a sudden husky laugh.

'I am… Just a bit,' she qualified, half under her breath, her own attention wholly captured by the wonder of his smile.

'It's a turn-on, *amore*,' he murmured huskily. 'But then I guess you know that.'

Thinking about all that she didn't know froze Misty for an instant, filled her with doubt, but then he lashed the lush pink peak of her breast with his tongue and closed his mouth over the straining tip and doubt vanished because there was no room for it any more. Indeed there was no room for anything but the raw intensity of her own driven response.

'We have all night…' Leone muttered hungrily, curving back from her to discard his boxers.

'I suppose…' She kept her eyes on his muscular chest. It was really going to happen. Her body was all heat and liquid eagerness but she was nervous: afraid it might hurt, afraid she might in some way betray her ignorance, for she did not want him to guess that he was about to become the only lover she had ever had.

After all, all he wanted was a casual tumble between the sheets, but *he* might start thinking that *she* wanted something more if he realised that she was a virgin. And, of course, she didn't. She was just madly attracted to him and that was that, and it was her own private business if she had decided that he would be her first lover. It didn't have to mean anything, she reasoned frantically with herself, fighting Birdie's moral conditioning with all her might, and it certainly didn't mean that she had special feelings for him. Developing special feelings for a male with Leone's reputation would be like shooting herself in the foot and she was far too sensible.

But as Leone drew her back to him with purposeful hands she met molten golden eyes and she burned and sense was nowhere to be found. He tasted her mouth and she trembled, her very skin feeling as though it were tightening over her bones, every inch of her taut and super sensitive.

'It's the way you look at me,' Leone confided with all male satisfaction. 'The way you react around me...it makes me *ache*...'

'I hated you...' Misty whispered in a tone of surprise, her mind refusing to comprehend how she had travelled from that violent hostility to the point where she could lie in his arms naked and it feel like the most natural thing in the world.

Leone ran light fingers through the silky tumble of hair spread across the pillow and gazed down at her as he let his other hand travel with caressing expertise up over her straining breasts. He watched her push herself up against his hand in an involuntary motion she could no more have resisted than she might have resisted the tide. Smouldering golden eyes surveyed her. 'You don't *now*...'

'No...' And conceding that reality scared Misty. In the space of days, he had somehow vanquished what had once been a certainty and she could not explain how or why.

But that possessive light in his stunning eyes was like a controlling forcefield surrounding her, shutting out everything she didn't want to acknowledge. The rapid beat of her own heart was leaving her breathless. The most enormous sense of excitement was penned up inside her, ready to break loose. The silence eddied in her ears, broken only by the ragged sigh of her own breath.

'I've never wanted anyone like this before,' she heard herself confide.

His eyes darkening, his lean bronzed features tautened and then suddenly he sunk one hand into her hair to raise her to him and he was ravishing her parted lips with his own again, letting his tongue delve into the moist interior of her mouth with explicit passion.

Her hunger came back at even stronger force. Her hands dug into his corded shoulders, loving the strength of him and the smoothness of his skin there. Indeed, for several intoxicating minutes she explored every part of him she could reach, but baulked at the most obvious.

'Touch me…' he urged raggedly.

And she was torn in two by excitement and nerves. He was hard and smooth and she was convinced there was far too much of him, but the fact that almost imperceptible tremors were running through his sleek, powerful frame empowered her. He groaned out loud with pleasure. She liked that: it meant she was doing things right. But before she could begin experimenting on him with greater daring, he pushed her back against the pillows and claimed a hungry, driving kiss.

'In the mood I'm in…a little goes a long way, *amore*…'

He lay half over her, playing sensually with her mouth while he toyed with the cluster of copper curls below her tensing tummy, slid her quivering thighs apart and traced the moist cleft at the heart of her. And from that point on she was all heat and electrified craving, every sensation driven by the aching tenderness there. He found the most sensitive spot and what remained of control was wrested from her with a vengeance. Her hips writhed and she sobbed out loud.

'Oh, please…'

'Waiting makes it better, *amore*,' Leone intoned against her parted lips as she sucked in breath like a drowning swimmer.

By the time he rose over her, sliding his hands beneath her squirming hips and pulling her to him, she was on fire with her own craving. He drove into her and a sharp rending pain momentarily gripped her, almost shocking her back to the real world again.

'You're so tight…' he groaned, gazing down at her with questioning eyes, a frown drawing his brows together. 'Am I hurting you?'

'Oh, no…' Misty hastened to assert through gritted teeth.

Leone surveyed her with veiled intensity and then he shifted with lithe power and eased himself very slowly and very gently deeper into her. '*Dio*…you feel incredible.'

The discomfort began to evaporate at the point where she was just about to tell him that she could not return the compliment. By then, she had taken all of him and was warming to the activity and the sensation so that by the time he began to move, she arched up and the frenzy of yearning desire flooded back to fill her almost in the same moment.

'I like it…'

Molten golden eyes collided with hers, sudden amusement flaring.

'With you,' she added jerkily.

He bent his dark head, brilliant eyes almost tender, and stole a lingering kiss. 'Sometimes you don't tell the whole truth.'

The excitement was rocketing again and, although she wanted to ask him what he meant by that, she couldn't find her voice. She moved under him, hot and abandoned, revelling in his sensual rhythm, letting the new wildness build inside her and pitch her higher and higher. His pace quickened and her heart slammed even faster, whimpers of sound torn from her while he drove her mindless with pleasure. At the furthest edge, she reached a climax of mind-blowing intensity, her entire body convulsed with fiery sensation and passion. He shuddered over her and ground out something in Italian and poured himself into her.

She held him close, conscious of a sweet, drowning pleasure in that simple act of closeness, acknowledging that in all her life she had never felt that close to another human being. In the circle of her arms, he felt as if he was hers and she loved that. He released her from his weight and then hauled her close again, holding her every bit as tight as she wanted to be held, and for a time neither of them said anything. Then he pushed her tumbled hair back from her pink face, gazed down into her softened grey eyes and then veiled his own.

'I've been thinking…I could help you trace your twin sister.'

At that suggestion coming out of nowhere at her at such a moment, Misty tensed in astonishment. 'Sorry?'

'Everyone ought to have family. It would only be a small favour…no big deal, *amore*.' Leone shifted a smooth brown shoulder in a slight dismissive shrug.

'No…nice thought but no, thanks,' Misty fielded tightly.

'Why not? Surely you want to meet her?'

'It's what *she* wants that counts and she's had my address and my phone number for four years now and she's done nothing with them,' Misty countered unsteadily. 'So just leave it.'

'I think you're scared—'

Inflamed by that comment, Misty pulled back from him. 'What would you know about it? I suppose you've read a few of those nice cosy stories where people went looking for long lost relatives and had a rapturous reunion…well, there's *nothing* nice and cosy in my background, just the hurt and damaged children our mum abandoned. There's three of us that I know of.'

Disconcerted by her fiery emotional reaction, Leone had thrust himself up against the pillows. Momentarily she was distracted. He looked gorgeous, she thought painfully, more gorgeous than ever with his black hair tousled and his stunning eyes reflecting the firelight, his olive skin dark and sexy and vibrant against the bed linen. In punishment for her own dismaying susceptibility, she turned her head away from him.

'You said, "three of us",' Leone reminded her. 'Three what?'

'Three sisters…maybe more, maybe boys too, for all I know!'

'Your mother had three children?'

'She married an older man when she was nineteen and she had a little girl by him. Social services told me that. Mum left him for my father but that didn't last and so Mum left my twin and I in care,' Misty advanced curtly.

'And?' Leone prompted as the strained silence dragged.

Her fine facial bones were prominent with rigidly re-strained emotion. 'I met Mum's ex-husband when I was going through my "tracing my roots" phase. You see, I thought he might really be my father…stupid of me. I mean, why would my twin and I have ended up in care if he had been?'

Leone said nothing. He reached out to close a hand over her taut, clenched fingers.

Disdaining his pity, Misty jerked her hand out of reach. 'Her ex-husband was still really bitter. He called Mum a slut and told me to get off his property. He said I was a fool to imagine that his daughter would want anything to do with the likes of me!'

'*Dio mio…*' Leone was pale beneath his bronzed skin, undoubtedly, she felt, wishing he had steered well clear of the subject of family.

'Birdie's my family,' Misty stated tightly. 'I was crazy to go searching and digging into Mum's past. All I got out of it was rejection and humiliation.'

Leone closed his hands over her arms and tipped her back to him, ignoring her stiff defensiveness to assert with emphasis, 'I'll *never* mention the idea again.'

But he had stirred up emotions that were not so easily set aside again. Feeling raw and needing to be alone, Misty rolled away from him and took refuge in the bathroom.

She turned on the bath taps because tears were trickling down her taut face and she was scared a sob might escape and carry back into the bedroom. Taken aback to see steam rising above the bath, she put the plug in and eventually clambered into the warm water. She sat hunched with her head bent over her knees, wishing the pain and the confusion that had by then stretched to encompass that wild bout of lovemaking with Leone would go away.

Why had she told him all those personal things? She was torn with regret and embarrassment. She had seen the shock and discomfiture flash through his gaze. And she didn't even blame him for that clumsy and naive offer of his to trace her twin. He had no concept of what it was like to come from her kind of background. He probably knew every member of his own family tree back a few generations at least. Weren't Italian families supposed to be really close?

Some time later, a knock sounded on the door. She ignored it. The door opened.

'I've used up all the hot water,' she told Leone fiercely without even looking up.

'I raided the drawing room downstairs for some brandy and Murdo caught me in the act,' Leone said in a grated undertone.

Involuntary amusement infiltrated her strained defences as she pictured what must have been an extraordinary scene. 'Oh, *dear*...'

'So the least you can do is drink it.'

'OK...I'll be out in a minute,' Misty promised, a reflective little smile chasing the tension away from her soft mouth. She might, she just *might* sugar his next coffee for him as a reward.

CHAPTER SIX

MISTY shifted and stretched sleepily. A whole series of unfamiliar little aches and pains assailed her, reminding her of the night that had passed. Leone...the warmth of memory uncoiled inside her and overpowered every other prompting. All she wanted to do was luxuriate in the cocoon of happiness that had begun building at some stage of the night hours.

But it was only a casual affair, Misty reminded herself hurriedly. She stifled the misgivings threatening to surface: the awareness that she didn't really know what she was doing, the worrying fact that she had allowed temptation to overrule her usual sense and caution. Wasn't she a grown woman and old enough to make her own decisions? Just for once in her life, she wanted to live for the moment and drink every second dry of its promise. And at that moment her world felt filled to overflowing with promise.

She opened her eyes. The curtains had been drawn back. Soft misty daylight was filtering in and Leone was by the window, his tall, powerful physique enhanced by a casual jacket worn with well-cut dark chinos. She studied him with helpless appreciation. He was terrific company and he was a total fantasy in bed...and in front of the fire...and other places too. How had she ever imagined that she hated him? Had she used that as a defence to hide behind? A way of denying the reality that she was hopelessly attracted to him? She was so grateful that he had brought down her barriers, so grateful that she hadn't missed out on feeling as good about herself as he had made her feel.

His cell phone buzzed and he dug it out and began to

talk in low-pitched urgent Italian. His tension pronounced, he paced a little. She finally saw his lean, strong face and, simultaneously, happiness began to seep out of her like water in a cracked jug. Leone looked grim. Grim as he had looked that day he had spelt out his proposition in the office at Brewsters without any shade of humour or indeed any hint of the male who had been behaving like a passionate lover with her only hours earlier.

The lovely warm sensations inside Misty started to shrivel. He had regrets, great big screaming regrets, she decided painfully. He had got out of bed, dressed and left her sleeping. With one notable exception, it was like all the books she had ever read, all the films she had ever seen that covered what a guy did after a one-night stand that he felt had been a mistake. And the exception? He was still in the same room, still in the same building. And why? In the circumstances, he was pretty much trapped.

Had he just looked at her in the light of day and wondered what on earth he had imagined he had seen in her? Or was he one of those hateful womanisers who lost interest the moment the chase was over? Not that the chase had lasted long, she conceded. Had he even chatted her up? She didn't think so. He had read her signals and just moved in for the kill. As one-night stands went, she had been a very easy lay. Even thinking about herself in that light hurt but there was a part of her all too eager to rub that pain and humiliation in hard. There she had been kidding herself on that she was in control of events, able to handle whatever happened, and the minute things went wrong she felt like death warmed over and sick with pain and rejection all over again.

'What time's breakfast?' she asked with studious casualness as he ended his call, fighting her own agonising sensitivity with all her might.

Leone jerked round, lean, strong face taut. For a split

second his raw tension was visible in the way he held himself and then his wide, sensual mouth curved into a faint smile. It was a forced smile and twelve hours earlier she could not have told the difference, but a lot had changed within that time frame.

'I'm afraid you've missed breakfast. It's almost one,' Leone informed her.

Misty was so disconcerted by that news that she sat up, but as the sheet fell below her breasts she snatched at it, suddenly very uncomfortable with her own bare skin in his presence. 'You should've woken me up!'

'What for? The obligatory fishing trip in the rain?'

'Sorry...?' Misty discovered that she could not quite bring herself to meet his gaze levelly and that her ability to concentrate was at an all-time low. Emotions were churning up inside her, raw, wounded feelings of shame and self-loathing exacerbated by growing anger. Why hadn't he left her alone? Had sleeping with her been his cruel way of bringing her down and punishing her for standing up to him? Was that the sort of guy he was? She didn't know any more, she didn't feel she knew *anything* any more, but her pride surged to the fore to conceal her mounting turmoil.

'The rest of the guests came up from the local hotel and most of them have gone down to the loch to fish. I gather it's tradition.'

She could hear the rain thumping against the window and barely suppressed a shudder.

'I said you were very tired after our extended journey yesterday—'

'You said...*what*?' Accidentally she looked at him.

'I don't like fishing,' Leone informed her with veiled eyes, no more keen, it seemed, than she to make head-on contact. In fact he sounded just a little desperate.

'I'd have thought you could've tolerated it for a few

hours…after all, you did come up here to stay with these people. Are the women fishing too?'

'Some of them.'

'I'm sure there's a pair of wellies I can borrow. A pity you didn't warn me about the fishing because I don't have anything suitable to wear.' Misty was struggling to keep her voice even. 'We must seem like the guests from hell. We arrive late, we nick the brandy and I'm still in bed the following afternoon.'

'Ted Garrison is a political power broker. His sole interest in our presence is how much cash I might contribute to his latest cause,' Leone informed her wryly. 'We could spend the entire weekend in bed and he wouldn't give a damn.'

'No offence intended, Leone,' Misty murmured with a bright smile pasted to her numb lips as she snatched up her nightdress and pulled it on. 'The sex was a great way of whiling away a boring evening, but let's not kid ourselves it would rise to the challenge of amusing us for a whole weekend!'

Leone was very still. As she escaped into the bathroom she contrived to steal a covert glance in his direction. His bold profile was rigid. He was surprised, of course he was. He hadn't expected her to get the punchline in first, but no way was she about to give him the ego boost of believing that the previous night had meant anything to her or that she had the smallest wish to repeat the experience. After washing her face, she saw tears in her eyes and she wrinkled her nose furiously. No matter if it killed her, she was going to pick herself up again and act as though nothing had happened.

When she emerged the bedroom was empty. She teamed a gossamer-fine lilac top ornamented with fine beading with the skirt that fell to mid-calf and a velvet-trimmed cardigan, brushed her hair until it fell into style and applied make-up. Time to get into role: she was the fake mistress, more interested in fashion and an ultra-feminine appearance than fishing and unlikely to dress for practicality even on a country weekend in a Scottish castle.

As she descended the winding stone staircase with care in her high heels, she caught the sound of chairs being scraped back followed by the murmur of voices receding from the hall below. Stepping down into the echoing front hall where a welcoming fire burned in the dimness but there appeared to be nobody else present, she hesitated for a moment and then a slight sound alerted her to the fact that she was not alone.

A distinguished-looking man with dark hair silvering at his temples stood just inside the entrance, an exasperated expression on his face as he removed a jacket dripping with raindrops. He glanced in her direction and then froze, a frownline lodged between his brows as he stared at her with narrowed eyes.

'Hi…' Misty coloured beneath the intensity of his appraisal, wondering if the outfit she had chosen looked that outlandish. 'Do you know where everyone has gone?'

'Into lunch, I would think. I was hoping I wasn't too late as the prospect of picnicking by the loch in this weather didn't appeal.' Treating her to a flirtatious smile, he strode forward to extend his hand. 'I'm Oliver Sargent.'

'Misty Carlton…' The instant she heard his name she recognised him, for he was Birdie's favourite politician, given to uttering the kind of homely sentiments that were most dear to her foster mother's heart.

His hand tightened on hers and then fell away as she spoke, but before she could wonder at his withdrawal a grey-haired older woman in country tweeds was advancing towards them.

'My goodness, Oliver, you look grey. Are you feeling all right? You had better change out of those wet clothes.'

GET FREE BOOKS and a FREE GIFT WHEN YOU PLAY THE...

SLOT MACHINE GAME!

Just scratch off the silver box with a coin. Then check below to see the gifts you get!

YES! I have scratched off the silver box. Please send me the 2 free Harlequin Presents® books and gift for which I qualify. I understand I am under no obligation to purchase any books, as explained on the back of this card.

306 HDL DRM9

106 HDL DRNQ
(H-P-10/02)

7	**7**	**7**	**Worth TWO FREE BOOKS plus a BONUS Mystery Gift!**
🍒	🍒	🍒	**Worth TWO FREE BOOKS!**
♣	♣	♣	**Worth ONE FREE BOOK!**
🔔	🔔	🍒	**TRY AGAIN!**

Visit us online at www.eHarlequin.com

DETACH AND MAIL CARD TODAY!

The Harlequin Reader Service® — Here's how it works:

Accepting your 2 free books and gift places you under no obligation to buy anything. You may keep the books and gift and return the shipping statement marked "cancel." If you do not cancel, about a month later we'll send you 6 additional novels and bill you just $3.57 each in the U.S., or $4.24 each in Canada, plus 25¢ shipping & handling per book and applicable taxes if any.* That's the complete price and — compared to cover prices of $4.25 each in the U.S. and $4.99 each in Canada — it's quite a bargain! You may cancel at any time, but if you choose to continue, every month we'll send you 6 more books, which you may either purchase at the discount price or return to us and cancel your subscription.

*Terms and prices subject to change without notice. Sales tax applicable in N.Y. Canadian residents will be charged applicable provincial taxes and GST.

If offer card is missing write to: Harlequin Reader Service, 3010 Walden Ave., P.O. Box 1867, Buffalo NY 14240-1867

BUSINESS REPLY MAIL
FIRST-CLASS MAIL   PERMIT NO. 717-003   BUFFALO, NY

POSTAGE WILL BE PAID BY ADDRESSEE

HARLEQUIN READER SERVICE
3010 WALDEN AVE
PO BOX 1867
BUFFALO NY 14240-9952

NO POSTAGE
NECESSARY
IF MAILED
IN THE
UNITED STATES

Without skipping a beat, the woman turned to Misty. 'I'm Peg Garrison. You can only be Misty. So nice to have some younger people staying for a change. I gather Leone has abandoned you—'

Misty tensed. 'Sorry?'

'Leone and Ted have taken a boat out on the loch. Ted called me on his cell phone. I doubt if we'll see them much before the party this evening. Ted rarely meets anyone as mad keen on fishing as he is himself, so he's sure to make the most of the opportunity.'

Taken aback by the content of that speech after what Leone had said on the same subject earlier, Misty found herself swept by her hostess into a chilly dining room where around a dozen older people were seated. She sat down and contemplated the minute portion of salad awaiting her.

'We always try to eat before we come,' her neighbour whispered with a rueful laugh. 'I believe you're staying here at the castle.'

'Yes.' Misty turned to smile at the faded blonde woman beside her.

'A mistake you'll only make once, as we did. The hotel is much more comfortable. I'm Jenny Sargent.'

'I think I met your husband out in the hall.'

'Oh, is Oliver back already? He's not very fond of fishing but Ted does rather expect one to share his favourite pursuits.'

'I'm Misty Carlton.'

'Is Misty short for something?' her neighbour continued chattily.

'Melissa, but I don't remember ever being called it,' Misty confided, tucking into her salad slowly in the hope of persuading her hungry stomach that it was a banquet, rather than a snack. She was picturing Leone on a boat in

the lashing rain and hoping he got seasick, soaked through
and had a thoroughly horrible afternoon.

Jenny's husband, Oliver, appeared midway through the
meal and sat down beside his hostess, who was giving
forth on how unnecessary central heating was while her
luncheon guests tried not to let their teeth chatter over their
miserly salads. Was Leone interested in politics? Misty
could not help wondering why on earth he had come to
stay for an entire weekend with such people. The other
guests were of a different generation and all the talk was
of politics, rather than business. Perhaps Leone wished to
engage political support in some matter which affected
Andracchi Industries, she thought vaguely.

On several occasions, she found Oliver Sargent skimming a glance in his wife's direction. At least she assumed
it was his wife he was looking at, for she could not imagine
why he should have any interest in her. Nonetheless, he
had the coldest grey eyes she had ever seen and she knew
that she would have to fib when she described him to
Birdie. He was such a smoothie and he flirted like mad
with every woman around him right under the nose of his
infinitely nicer wife. But she would tell her foster mother
that he was an absolute charmer rather than disappoint her.

Lunch was followed by a tour of Castle Eyrie's every
room. Misty was surprised to find much of Peg Garrison's
running commentary on the history of the castle directed
at herself, although she was certainly interested. It was a
fortified tower house with three storeys that had been al-
tered several times over the centuries so that various stair-
cases ran off in odd directions and corridors had ninety-
degree turns, but the panelled rooms and casement
windows had enormous charm and she thought it was sad
that the Garrisons had neglected their summer home to
such an extent.

'Now that the children have flown the nest, it's too large

for us and we intend to buy a villa in the South of France,' her hostess informed her.

'Is Leone interested in buying this place?' Jenny asked in some surprise when Peg Garrison had moved away. 'I shouldn't have thought that it was his cup of tea. Oliver...?'

Her husband approached them with a stiff smile.

'I was just saying to Misty. Peg seems to think that Leone's gasping to acquire a Scottish castle.'

'Perhaps he is...' As Oliver Sargent treated his artless wife to a frowning glance that made the kindly older woman redden Misty found herself warming even less to the man and was glad when his attention was claimed by someone else.

'We got to know Leone through his younger sister...a tragic business that,' Jenny Sargent sighed in continuance. 'Battista was working for Oliver at the time. She was a delightful girl. Young people and fast cars...such a dangerous combination. Leone was devastated when she died.'

'Yes.' Misty was recalling the ashen colour Leone had turned just squeezing out the admission that that pretty girl in the portrait was his late sister and she realised that Battista must have been killed in a car accident.

'I'm afraid Leone's avoided us ever since and I don't blame him for it,' Jenny asserted, her sympathy clear in her homely face. 'I'm sure whenever he sees Oliver and I, it brings back unfortunate memories of the last few weeks of Battista's life.'

Misty was finding it harder and harder to smile and chat and it was a relief when the gathering broke up. Her wretched subconscious was betraying her by serving up images of the night before: Leone laughing about being caught helping himself to the brandy and his promise to Murdo that he would replace the entire bottle first thing in the morning. She had been surprised that Leone had realised that Murdo was afraid of being accused of having a secret tipple and losing his job, and touched that the younger man had cared.

She had never dreamt that such an extraordinary passion could exist or that she could feel anything with such intensity. Being with him had felt so special but the cold light of day had been harsh and revealing. Or had it been? Had her own fear of rejection led her into overreaction? Wasn't it possible that Leone's forbidding aspect might have related to something that had nothing to do with her? Even that phone call which he had been in the midst of making? Well, she had jumped and that was that and it was for the best, wasn't it?

Warmth greeted her as she opened their bedroom door. A log fire was roaring in the grate and Leone was standing in front of it, shivering and drenched to the skin. As that was exactly what she had hoped on his behalf some hours earlier, she was infuriated by the instant charge of concern that filled her. His black hair curling with damp, his lean, bronzed features still wet, his shimmering golden eyes assailed hers.

'Did you mean what you said earlier?' Leone demanded with stark clarity.

Disconcerted, Misty trembled and angled back against the door to close it. As her gaze centred on him in a frantic search for some lead on how to answer that question her heart began to thump inside her like an overwound clock, racing and then threatening to stop altogether. In the fierce set of his darkly handsome features she could see how much was riding on her response and that shook her.

'*Dio mio*…you *didn't* mean it!' Leone ground out with a flash of his even white teeth, shooting her a look of raw anger. 'So why did you say it?'

Her triangular face had drained of colour and her knees

had developed a slight wobble but her chin came up. 'I got the impression that if I didn't say it, you would.'

'I wouldn't be that crude,' Leone sliced back at her, strong jawline at an aggressive angle. 'You talked like you were a whore!'

Colour drenched her cheekbones. 'I—'

'I don't want to hear you speaking like that again,' Leone cut in.

Misty bridled.

'How would you feel if I had spoken to you in that manner?' Leone demanded.

Gutted, she thought inwardly, her mind a sea of confusion that such a dialogue was even taking place between them. He still wanted her...he *still* wanted her. Indeed he cared enough to challenge her rejection of him. A whoosh of warmth at that knowledge surged up through her, wiping away the cold, sick feeling of having been used that she had fought to suppress all afternoon.

'Let me get you a towel,' she said unevenly.

Leone gritted something in Italian that sounded very rude.

'Don't swear at me,' Misty told him defensively.

'I wasn't swearing. I was telling you...don't *ever* do that to me again.'

'OK.'

Leone spoke again just as she reached the bathroom door. 'I would have hurt you less if you'd warned me that you were a virgin.'

Entirely unprepared for that sally, Misty spun round, pink flooding her cheeks. 'I—'

'I would've mentioned it last night but you seemed keen to conceal the fact.'

Misty met level dark golden eyes of enquiry and muttered, 'I was embarrassed.'

'I was stunned but very pleased that you chose me,' Leone murmured huskily. 'Yet with what I believed that I knew about you—'

'Flash and I shared the same foster home for years. We were more like brother and sister.'

Leone smiled. 'But you were engaged to Redding—'

'Not for very long and, really, that's none of your business,' Misty told him in a chagrined rush.

'Did you honestly think that I was complaining?' As she tried to step past Leone he caught her to him and claimed a drowning kiss, his sensual mouth hungry and demanding on hers, and the world spun crazily around her, her tummy clenching on the surge of raw desire. Her fingers closed into his wet jacket and began to drag it off him as she pushed into the hard, muscular heat of him. With a roughened laugh, he released her and disposed of the jacket himself. He backed her up against the bed and closed her back into his arms to lift her and bring her down on the mattress.

'I've got to get ready for the party—'

His stunning golden eyes darkened and veiled. 'Do you really want to go?'

'Leone…' Heart hammering but thoughts bewildered, Misty looked up at him and let her shoes fall off her feet. 'Of course we have to go—'

'There's no, "of course" about anything, *amore*.'

'Except when it comes to how you behave in someone else's home,' Misty muttered, watching him peel off his damp shirt, eyes widening on the breathtaking expanse of his bronzed hair-roughened chest. Just looking at him made her own body clench tight. She felt out of control, out of control of both thought and response.

Leone ran slow, provocative hands up her long, slender legs, lifting her skirt out of his path, and then he came to the lace-topped stockings held up with suspenders and expelled his breath in a sudden groan of appreciation. 'That is *so* sexy…'

'And you're *so* predictable…'

To try and prove her wrong, he bent his arrogant dark head over her and ran his tongue along the bare skin above the stocking tops. She managed a muffled giggle but damp heat flowered at the very heart of her and made her shiver. He tugged her up, extracted her from her cardigan and top and kissed her with deep, erotic thoroughness in the midst of the exercise.

'*Santo Cielo*…I need to be inside you,' he growled with ragged urgency, coming down on the bed still half clothed, dealing with her lingerie in a most summary fashion.

An uninhibited moan was wrenched from her as he found the slick wet heat between her thighs. His unhidden urgency only made her more wild for him. Aching with the same driving need, she angled up to him and at last he was there, plunging into her heated core with a delicious force that made her cry out. His driving thrusts sent electrifying excitement leaping through her and the fierce storm of his possession sent her flying to an ecstatic peak and wave after wave of shattering pleasure.

Sitting up, Leone began to peel her out of her remaining clothes, pausing every now and then to caress her with expert hands, shocking her with the speed with which he could rouse her again. She ran her fingers through his black hair, curved them to his blue-shadowed jawline, reached up and found his mouth for herself with new confidence. She couldn't stop touching him but that felt all right because he was doing the exact same thing, but deep down inside she now knew what made him special and the strength of her own emotions frightened her…

*   *   *

So what *did* you do this afternoon?' Leone enquired as they crossed the landing to go downstairs later that evening.

Misty smoothed down the glorious white halter-neck dress she wore and glanced up at his lean, strong face with a teasing smile. 'I lunched…in a very small way, got the official tour of the castle…it's *really* beautiful, Leone. Oh, yes, and I got to meet Oliver Sargent—'

The hand Leone had at her narrow spine tensed. 'You can't have done. Oliver was on the other boat and it stayed out on the loch all afternoon—'

'He must have sneaked off it because he came back just as I arrived downstairs.'

Leone had fallen still and he stared down at her with narrowed eyes as dark as a midnight sky, his beautiful bone structure taut. 'Friendly, was he?'

'At first…and then, no, not really,' Misty framed uncomfortably, wondering what was the matter with him. 'I much preferred his wife.'

'You met her as well?' Leone breathed in a harsh undertone.

'Aren't they friends of yours?'

'No.'

'Did you expect me to skulk in the bedroom for the rest of the day just because you weren't here?' Misty asked.

'No.' Hard jawline clenched, Leone shrugged a wide shoulder with something less than his usual fluidity of movement. 'It's not important. Forget it.'

Of course, hadn't Jenny Sargent remarked that she suspected that Leone avoided them because they roused painful memories of his sister, Battista? And true to that belief, Leone was pale beneath his olive skin. Compassion stirred in Misty and her defensive stance evaporated. She wondered how long it had been since his sister had died and

decided it must have been a fairly recent event for him
still to be that sensitive.

It was a very big party and their first stop was the buffet
laid on by the caterers. A large room had been cleared for
dancing and adorned with beautiful flower arrangements.
Misty drifted round the floor in Leone's arms, trying not
to wonder where their affair could be going, reminding
herself that no relationship came with guarantees. But she
knew that for the first time in three years she was falling
in love again, and that terrified her for it seemed to her
that they had started out all wrong and she wished that she
could go back and have a second chance.

An hour into the party she caught her shoe in the hem
of her dress and went upstairs to pin it up. When she came
back down again, Oliver Sargent stepped into her path. 'I'd
like to offer you a friendly word of warning.'

His voice was slightly slurred, as if he had been drinking
too much, and lines of strain were grooved between his
nose and mouth.

'What about?' Misty frowned at him.

'Get out of Leone Andracchi's life,' the older man told
her in a grim undertone. 'You can't trust him. He's *only*
using you!'

Stunned by those daunting assurances from a man she
barely knew, Misty stared at Oliver Sargent, but he immediately turned away and moved back into the crush.
Now what was she supposed to make of that? It was obvious that the enmity between Leone and the older man
was mutual. But why should she have been dragged into
the midst of it?

CHAPTER SEVEN

IN THE early hours of the following morning, Misty lay watching Leone sleep.

Dawn light fingered across the bed, playing across his stunning dark features, highlighting the ridiculous length of his black lashes, moving on to rest on the relaxed line of his wide, sensual mouth. In such a short space of time he had become so important to her, but what sort of closeness did they have when she did not feel she could share Oliver Sargent's warning and ask why the older man should have approached her with such chilling advice?

But then what level of closeness did she expect when she and Leone had only been together for so short a time? Wasn't she being unreasonable? After all, Oliver Sargent had been drinking heavily and, if he didn't like Leone, he might simply have been trying to cause trouble. All the same, there had been something surprisingly sincere about the older man's manner, some quality that had spooked her. But then the man was a politician and made his living by being convincing, she reminded herself in exasperation, and she went back to studying Leone with possessive pleasure.

'I need to know where we're going in this relationship,' Misty admitted in the limo that was ferrying her and Leone back to the London apartment that afternoon.

The silence stretched like a treacherous swamp.

Inky black lashes screening his gaze, Leone murmured, 'I can't answer that yet.'

Misty drew in a slow, steadying breath but she had lost

colour. 'I won't be your mistress. I assume that I am still working for you…?'

Leone tensed and took a moment to consider that angle, which suggested to her that that role of hers was no longer as cut and dried as it had once been. 'Yes.'

'And you still have no plans to tell me what this grand pretence is all about?'

Leone assessed her taut face. 'No, not at present.'

'Then we go back to strictly business terms,' Misty decreed without hesitation.

Leone settled smouldering golden eyes on her, his incredulity patent. '*Porca miseria!* That would be ridiculous!'

'I won't feel comfortable with any other arrangement. You can't have it both ways,' Misty warned him, a sick, sinking sensation infiltrating her stomach.

'Blackmail just makes me more stubborn,' Leone spelt out sardonically.

Misty reddened. 'I am *not* blackmailing you!'

'I'll be in New York for the next week. Think it over while I'm away.'

As that unexpected little speech sank in, she realised that she was dealing with a master of one-upmanship. The mere thought of him vanishing for an entire seven days while matters stood unresolved between them was a body-blow. How had he got her that dependent so fast? She slung him a suspicious look, grey eyes silvering with a volatile mix of anxiety and resentment. 'I shan't miss you.'

'You sound as if you're about seven years old, *amore*.' Leone closed his hand over her coiled fingers where they rested on the seat between them. 'Why are you so keen to screw up something that's working?'

'Maybe it's not working quite as well for me,' Misty breathed stiltedly, but she held on to his hand.

She spent the first half of the following week with Birdie

and Leone phoned her twice. She was accustomed to busy days and the long hours were empty when she returned to London. On the penultimate night when she found herself watching the phone like a clingy, desperate woman, she made herself go out to the cinema. It was only when she was on the brink of falling asleep that evening that she realised that her period was several days late. Assuming that her emotional ups and downs had upset her cycle, she put the matter back out of her mind without concern.

Leone called her at two in the morning and she came awake with a sleepy sigh, defences at their lowest ebb as she listened to his rich, dark drawl and her toes stretched and curled.

'My flight will get in at seven,' Leone murmured tautly.

'Tonight?'

'In a few hours.'

'Oh…' In the darkness she smiled and smiled.

'So go back to sleep,' Leone instructed huskily. 'When you wake up, I'll be there.'

It sounded wonderful but she woke up again after five. Excitement had got her adrenalin going and, after wrestling with a cautious wish to play everything very cool, she finally gave way to what she really wanted to do and decided to meet him at the airport. By that stage, time was of the essence and she dressed at speed in casual white flared jeans and a vibrant turquoise top.

The cab she called picked her up late and she had to run through the airport. She was about twenty feet away when she saw Leone emerging into the concourse. Falling to a breathless halt, she thrust her streaming copper hair back from her face and waited for him to see her. He looked preoccupied and forbidding but stunningly attractive. And then he glanced in her direction and froze, what could only be described as an aghast look flashing across his lean, strong face.

As Misty read that unwelcome response to her appearance, she spun away in an uncoordinated surge and began to head fast in the opposite direction. A split second later, the world round her exploded into sudden noise and activity. A camera flashed, momentarily blinding her into a stumbling halt. Loud voices were shouting at her. She backed away in shock and confusion, truly not understanding what was happening, her mind far more full of the appalled expression Leone had betrayed when he'd recognised her and frozen in anguish on that image.

'Did you know Oliver Sargent was—?' a man demanded urgently, only to be drowned out by another, who yelled, 'Miss Carlton…how do you feel about what you've just learned? Angry? Bitter?'

Yet another camera focused on her as she kept on backing and backing away from the band of shouting men surrounding her. And then suddenly Leone was breaking through the crush, snatching the camera from the man waving it in her face and throwing it aside in a violent gesture that took her even more aback.

'Get the hell away from her!' Leone launched, hauling her under one powerful arm and immediately curving her round to shelter her with his body and prevent the intrusive lenses from capturing a shot of her shell-shocked face.

'What's going on?' she demanded.

A couple of big musclebound men waded in to clear their path and Leone urged her away from the fracas at speed.

'One of those journalists mentioned Oliver Sargent!' she gasped.

But there was no time for explanations. The paparazzi gave chase and when Misty and Leone finally reached the security of the limousine, Misty had a stitch in her side and couldn't find the breath to speak.

'It didn't occur to me that you'd come to meet me this

early in the morning,' Leone admitted with fierce regret. 'The press were waiting to ask me for my comments. The minute I saw you I realised all hell was about to break loose. Are you all right?'

'Please just tell me what's happening.' Misty raised an unsteady hand to her damp brow where a headache was beginning to pound, but she was relieved to appreciate that his discomfiture at her appearance at the airport had not been the rejection that she had read it as being.

'A tabloid newspaper is breaking a big story today and it involves you.'

Misty stared at him with rounded eyes. 'How on earth could it involve me? You mean, it's some story to do with you and I somehow got dragged in?'

'No…' His strong bone structure taut beneath his olive skin, Leone was choosing his words with visible care. 'A friend tipped me off while I was still in New York. He emailed a copy of the lead article…'

Leone extended a folded newspaper to her. 'I'm sorry…I'm sorrier than I have ever been about anything.'

What did Leone have to be sorry about? Misty shook the paper open and just gaped at the front page. Above a picture of her taken the night of the film première ran the words, IS THIS OLIVER SARGENT'S LONG LOST DAUGHTER?

'Where did this rubbish come from?' Misty regarded the headline and the smaller inset picture of the politician she had met at Castle Eyrie with wide eyes of incredulity.

'Without DNA testing, no such claim can be proved,' Leone breathed. 'But on the basis of the information that I have, there is a very high degree of probability that Sargent *is* your natural father.'

Together those two statements of fact cut through the fog of Misty's disbelief and focused her mind again. She stared back at him in horror, for initially all she could recall was her almost instinctive recoil from the suave older man. 'You honestly believe that this crazy story *might* be true?'

Dark eyes without the merest shimmer of gold rested on her, his level of strain palpable. 'Yes.'

Yes? And with that one little word everything Misty had known about herself seemed to collapse and shatter. When she had been much younger, she had often wondered who her father was, but since her late mother had refused to name him even to the social services she had accepted that she had no hope of ever finding out. So what could be more devastating than the discovery that a newspaper knew more about her parentage than she did herself?

The paper still lay on her lap unopened. Leone had been forewarned and must already have read it. She felt horribly humiliated and she was deep in shock. Could there be truth in such a wild allegation? Could Oliver Sargent have had a relationship with her mother all those years ago?

Her hand trembling, she began to open the newspaper.

'Leave it until we get back to the house,' Leone advised.

'House?' Misty queried.

'By now your apartment will be beseiged by the press. I can protect you better in my own home.'

She studied Leone, noting his low-key delivery and the gravity etched into every line of his lean, powerful face. He was trying to help and support her and, while on one level she was grateful, on another she was cringing with embarrassment. 'You came back early from New York because of this,' she said tightly. 'I'm sorry.'

'You have nothing to be sorry about,' Leone stated with unexpected harshness. 'I caused this.'

How had he caused it? By putting her in the public eye? By making her a source of interest to the press? Perhaps it was more her own fault, she thought numbly: she had refused to talk to the journalists who had initially contacted

her. Had she given a few facts about herself, possibly nobody would have bothered to check out who she was in
any greater depth. But how had anyone managed to establish what she had been unable to find out even for herself?
Her brain still refused to come to grips with that headline.
How *could* she be Oliver Sargent's daughter? And what
were the odds against her having actually met the man face
to face only a week ago? That had surely been the most
amazing coincidence.

'Don't read that rubbish.' As Misty bent her head to
scrutinise the newspaper article, Leone stretched out a lean
brown hand and flipped it off her lap again.

'What are you doing?' Misty asked in bewilderment.

'Tabloids always sensationalise stories. Don't waste
your time.'

Involuntarily, she closed her eyes and swallowed hard.
She knew she would read it all and chew over every sen-
tence, but she felt it might be wiser to do that without
Leone as an audience. It had to be a pretty awful article
if he was so keen to prevent her from seeing it.

Leone curved a protective arm round her and swept her
up the steps of a big tall house before she could even get
a proper look at it. Her bemused gaze darted over the spacious, elegant hall and then returned inexorably to the
newspaper that Leone had in his other hand. 'I've *got* to
see it,' she told him.

With a reluctance she could feel he extended it again.

'Let's go upstairs.' Pausing to address the hovering
manservant in Italian, Leone led her towards the imposing
staircase. 'We'll have some breakfast. I don't know about
you but I'm hungry.'

'Yeah…' Misty couldn't have eaten to save her life, but
she followed his lead, striving to behave as though the
world she knew had not exploded beneath her feet.

'Try to understand that the press are much more interested in roasting Oliver Sargent alive in print than in your angle on this...try not to take it personally,' Leone urged.

At that piece of well-meant advice, Misty had to swallow the hysterical giggle tickling at the back of her dry throat. Why was it that men always shied away from the emotional fall-out of any event and concentrated on the practicalities? Did he really believe that even at her age she could find out from a newspaper that her father might be a famous politician and *not* take it personally?

'Sargent has made a lot of enemies in the media,' Leone continued with determination, shepherding her into a charming reception room already bright with early morning sunlight. 'They're out to get him, not you.'

Misty recalled reading one of Oliver Sargent's stern homilies on the number of babies being born out of wedlock and the effect that that had on society and on the children themselves. The older man was often both attacked and applauded for his moral stance. She could see that the revelation that he had fathered illegitimate children of his own and abandoned both them and their mother to their fate would crown him as the ultimate hypocrite in the eyes of many.

'I don't want you to get upset over this.' Leone's Sicilian accent had thickened to charge every syllable he spoke with the strength of his feelings.

Absorbing the first few saccharine-sweet sentences and the spread of pictures within the newspaper, Misty realised with shrinking discomfiture that she was to figure as an object of pity to the reader. Oliver Sargent's opulent country home was depicted beside the small terraced house where Misty had been fostered before being sent to Fossett's.

'Your mother's first husband was a generation older than she was. He was a college professor,' Leone stated without any inflection at all before she could get any deeper into the article. 'He encouraged her to enroll in further education classes. Sargent was a law student at the same university.'

'I can't imagine my mother studying,' Misty mumbled, already cringing with hurt at seeing in print the statement that she had been a troubled child, who had often played truant from school. It was true but she had become a regular attender after going to live at Fossetts at the age of twelve.

'The affair only became public knowledge when her husband discovered through hospital tests that you and your twin couldn't be his children. Your mother ran to Sargent for support but he turned his back on her. He had been engaged to Jenny all along.'

Misty thought of the pleasant woman she had met at Castle Eyrie and her stomach gave a protesting somersault. Jenny Sargent was about to discover that her husband had fathered another woman's children during their engagement. She too would feel betrayed and bitter and terribly hurt.

In the article, Misty's unhappy and rootless childhood was compared to Oliver Sargent's life of affluence and privilege, and she was skimming through that character assassination with an innate sense of distaste when she came on a section that turned her skin clammy. Her broken engagement to Philip was mentioned. 'Philip ditched Misty after she found out that she couldn't have kids a supposed and anonymous friend of hers had revealed.

'No…' A stricken moan was wrenched from Misty as she absorbed that cruel public exposure of her own biggest secret. She felt sick to the stomach.

Dragging the newspaper from her, Leone closed his arms round her trembling length. In hurt and shame and the agonising thought of him having read those same lines, she pulled away from him and a tearing sob escaped her.

'Go *away*…' she told him chokily. 'Let me deal with this by myself.'

But Leone was persistent. With a fierce objection in his own language, he tugged her back to him and he was too strong for her to resist. She could no longer restrain the great swell of tumultous emotion attacking her and the tears fell thick and fast. She could have borne the storm of Oliver Sargent being her putative father, for that still seemed quite unreal to her, but the painful reality of her own inability to conceive being put into print was more than she could stand.

'*Per amor di Dio*…I couldn't protect you from this. It was too late.' His rich dark drawl roughened with raw regret, Leone crushed her into the hard, muscular heat of his big, powerful body. 'Don't let yourself be hurt by it.'

Misty lifted welling eyes to his charged gaze, recognising the ferocious tension written into his devastatingly handsome dark features. 'I don't want you involved in this mess,' she confessed. 'That only makes me feel worse!'

'I *am* involved. I'm involved a great deal more than you appreciate.' Leone stared down at her with haunted dark eyes, ashen pale below his bronzed skin.

Misty assumed that he was blaming himself for putting her in the public eye in the first place and she shook her copper head in vehement objection, silken strands of bright hair flying back from her taut cheekbones. 'That's not true.'

'Everything in that newspaper story only emphasises what a very special woman you are,' Leone asserted with conviction.

'It is *so* special to be infertile,' Misty launched back at him in bitter pain. 'Oh, yes, *so* special!'

Tearing herself free of him in shamed and chagrined regret at having let that revealing response escape her, Misty spun away, but long, lean fingers closed over hers and entwined, preventing her from putting any real distance between them.

'That doesn't matter to me,' Leone insisted with harsh emphasis.

As Misty snatched in a sobbing breath, she could have wept in receipt of that assurance. Why on earth *should* it matter to him? After all, he wasn't thinking of marrying her. But, regardless of that reality, she recognised that she had still not wanted Leone to know her secret. She had feared that, just like her former fiancé, he might start thinking of her as being something less than other women.

He eased her back to him and the last of her prickly, independent defences subsided. She loved him, she loved him even more for being there for her when so many men leapt for cover at the first sign of trouble or embarrassment. Closing her arms round him in acceptance, she looked up at him, grey eyes silver with emotion. 'Make love to me,' she whispered softly.

Betraying disconcertion, Leone tensed. 'Misty, I…'

Misty turned white and thrust him back from her in such sudden rebuttal she took him by surprise. 'Forget it,' she urged strickenly.

In the act of stalking to the door, she was lifted bodily off her feet and up into Leone's strong arms. '*Santo Cielo!* How could you think that I don't want you? I wanted you every hour of every day I was away from you!' he grated rawly.

Relief travelled through Misty in a winging, weakening surge. At that moment, she had never been more desperate to lose herself in his passion and know that, regardless of those cheap tabloid revelations, he still found her attractive.

'But we have to talk first,' Leone completed in a hoarse undertone.

'Later…nothing else matters right now.'

'Misty—'

'Shut up,' she told him, reaching up in a desperate movement to cover that wide sensual mouth with her own.

With a feeling groan, he took her invitation with fierce urgency. He crossed the landing and shouldered his path into a bedroom furnished in masculine shades of green. There he laid her down on the wide divan bed and stood over her, lean, strong face taut. 'Are you sure about this?' he asked thickly.

'Well, if you want to have breakfast first, I'll understand,' Misty quipped unevenly.

His cell phone was buzzing. He switched it off and tossed it aside with heartening indifference, his smouldering golden eyes reluctant to leave hers for a second. What he said about the possibility of breakfast was short and succinct.

Misty was working really hard at not thinking about that newspaper story and Oliver Sargent. But it was impossible for her not to recall how the man who might be her own father had attempted to come between her and Leone by warning her that she could not trust the younger man. Now that she saw the most likely motivation for that approach, she was appalled. From the instant she'd given her name, Oliver Sargent would have known who she was and he had seen her as a threat to his precious reputation. His own behaviour virtually confirmed that he believed her to be his daughter. Had he assumed that she knew who he was too?

A shiver ran through Misty. She was seeing wheels within wheels and it scared her. At that point, another stab of comprehension assailed her and she turned dazed eyes on Leone. 'You knew all along that I might be Oliver Sargent's daughter!' she exclaimed to the male poised by the bed watching her every change of expression. 'Somehow you discovered that when you were having me checked out…didn't you?'

Wearing something of the aspect of a male in the dock on a murder charge, Leone nodded in confirmation, his tension pronounced.

'That's okay,' Misty assured him gently, eyes soft beneath her lashes, for even as she had spoken she was remembering Leone's equally offbeat behaviour that same weekend. He could have had no idea that Oliver Sargent would be visiting Castle Eyrie too and he had attempted to keep her and her putative father apart. Leone had been shocked when he had learned that she had already met the older man and had endeavoured without success to persuade her that there had been no need for them to go downstairs and attend the party that evening.

'I don't want to talk about this any more,' she confided unsteadily. 'There's no point. Now that I know the truth, I can see that Oliver Sargent was scared just being in the same room as me that weekend. But I've done without a father all my life and I'm hardly gasping for one now. *His* loss, not mine.'

Grave as a stone statue, Leone stared at her, and then he came down on the bed beside her and gathered her close. 'But you've been hurt so much by this.'

Her eyes watered and she mock-punched a wide muscular shoulder, tempted to tell him that nothing really mattered as long as she had him, that she could stand *anything* as long as she had him, but too cautious to risk such a frank confession. 'Stop being so wet!' she told him instead and she pushed him backwards, taking him by surprise so that he fell across the bed.

Startled, Leone looked up at her, brilliant golden eyes shimmering over her smiling face. 'You're a hell of a woman, *bella mia.*'

'Yeah…' Leaning over him, Misty tugged loose his tie

and trailed it off. 'And since you're being so shy about getting your kit off, I'm about to do it for you!'

'I hate to keep on repeating myself…but we *do* need to talk,' Leone framed half under his breath.

'You've stopped fancying me, haven't you?' Misty whispered jaggedly, all the colour draining from her tightening features.

Leone reached up and meshed long fingers into her hair before she could retreat from him again, and with his other hand he dragged hers down to the iron-hard thrust of his arousal beneath the tailored cloth of his trousers. 'Sorry to be so graphic but I'm always in this condition around you.'

Misty trembled in receipt of that proof. 'Always?'

'If I'd known what your ex-fiancé had done to you three years ago, I'd have torn that little creep limb from limb when I met him!' Leone ground out.

Reassured, Misty embarked on his shirt buttons. 'It's been a long time since I had any regrets in that line.'

Leone sat up and wrenched himself free of his jacket. 'Move in with me.'

At that sudden invitation, Misty stared at him in astonishment.

'I've never asked a woman that before,' he admitted with equally staggering abruptness.

It seemed obvious to her that Leone was unsure of the offer he had just made. She was shaken that he could be that impulsive, hurt that he could not hide his uncertainty from her, and she forced a determined laugh. 'I'd have to know you a lot longer before I would even consider moving to London on your behalf.'

She watched the disconcertion flare in his gorgeous eyes. He was so proud, so arrogant that her apparent amusement had flicked his ego on the raw. 'I'm not letting you go back to Norfolk.'

'The whole world doesn't turn at your convenience,'

Misty told him teasingly, and then he lifted her off him and rolled her under him instead. As he pried her lips apart with the plunging, ravishing heat of his sensual mouth she learned that her body turned and burned at his first passionate touch.

'I've had nothing but cold showers all week,' he groaned against her reddened lips.

He slid off the bed with pronounced reluctance and began to undress with all the hot impatience of a very aroused male. Just watching him did crazy things to her heartbeat. She wriggled out of her jeans, raised her arms, arched her spine and peeled off her top.

'You get to take off the rest...you're so good at it.' Misty reclined back against the pillows, confident that she was wanted, self-esteem restored.

Brilliant golden eyes set beneath spiky black lashes sought out hers. 'I was just practising for you coming along.'

Involuntarily, Misty giggled. 'I've heard some excuses in my time but that one is priceless!'

'You're so resilient.' Leone studied her with flattering fascination. 'I thought you'd still be coming apart at the seams over that tabloid story.'

He came down on the bed, all bronzed vibrant flesh, rippling muscles and magnificent arousal, and her mouth ran dry and she melted from inside out in response. No, she was not about to come apart at the seams while she had Leone in a supportive role, she conceded to herself without hesitation. She shivered as he released the catch on her bra, moaned out loud as he shaped the pouting swell of her breasts. She felt so sensitive there that the smallest touch on her taut nipples burned like fire through the rest of her and she blushed like mad.

'I ought to get points for appreciating how beautiful you

were when you were trying to hide your glory in shapeless suits the colour of concrete,' Leone informed her thickly.

'I never felt beautiful in my life until you looked at me,' Misty confided with helpless honesty.

He spread her like a willing sacrifice on the bed and worked his sensual path down over her straining breasts to her quivering tummy and, disposing swiftly of her panties, to the very heart of her. Her body ached for him with such immediacy that anything less than instant fulfilment literally hurt. Within minutes, she was lost in a sensual daze of writhing, gasping abandonment. She clutched at his hair, his shoulders and then gave herself wholly up to the voluptuous pleasure of what he was doing to her. Her climax took her like a tidal wave sweeping her to an explosive peak of hot, shattering delight that seemed to last for ever.

'I hope you don't have to go away any time soon again,' Misty mumbled in the aftermath.

'I missed you too, *amore*...' Leone drove into her with tender force and she closed her eyes again and let the wicked wanton pleasure take her by storm.

He pushed her to the heights again and it was wild and wonderful. Arching up to him, she matched his fluid thrusts and sobbed out loud when the frenzy of hunger controlled her afresh. But when that sweet, drowning passion of both body and senses engulfed her again, she came out of the experience with tears stinging her eyes, feeling that they had been closer than they had ever been and full of dreaming happiness.

Leone expelled his breath in a ragged hiss and kissed her and held her rather too tight for comfort. 'Now we're going to go and have breakfast and talk...and you're going to promise me that you'll reserve judgement until I've finished speaking.'

What on earth did he wish to talk about? His invitation

for her to move in with him? What else could it be? Why the heck had she assumed that that was an impulsive suggestion? After all, Leone was not the impulsive type. Indeed, most of the time, Leone gave her the impression of being the sort of male who planned everything right down to the final full stop. Furthermore, as he had been referring to their need to have a serious talk since they'd arrived at his house, it was much more likely that the idea of her moving in with him had been on his mind while he'd been in New York...

CHAPTER EIGHT

IN THE imposing dining room on the ground floor, Misty made an exaggerated show of sugaring Leone's coffee.

'Do you think you could be serious for a few minutes?'

Misty focused on Leone with ruefully amused eyes. She reckoned he looked serious enough for both of them but she couldn't concentrate. Only a couple of hours earlier she had believed that her world had fallen apart, but now, even though she knew she had still to deal with what she had learned about Oliver Sargent, her most overriding sensation was one of bubbling contentment.

The manservant whisked the metal cover from the breakfast fry she had cheerfully ordered. But as the familiar aroma of the bacon hit her nostrils, something quite unfamiliar happened to her digestive system. Attacked by an instant wave of nausea, Misty lurched out of her seat and bolted for the cloakroom.

Leone hammered on the door she had bolted behind her. 'Are you all right?'

Clutching the vanity basin to stay upright, Misty surveyed her drawn face in the mirror and suppressed a groan. Her tummy was still rolling and she felt rather dizzy too. Grimacing, she freshened up, thinking that it was just typical that she should succumb to some nasty, embarrassing bug at the very moment when she wished to look and feel her best.

Emerging again to receive Leone's questioning scrutiny, Misty said with determined brightness, 'I'm really not that hungry.'

'Are you feeling ill?'

'Of course I'm not feeling ill.' Misty was grateful that she had put some blusher on her cheeks and renewed her lipstick.

Back at the dining table, she sipped her cup of tea. 'You were about to get serious,' she reminded him cheerfully.

Leone had not touched his own breakfast and his strong bone structure was clenched hard. 'First, I want to tell you about my sister, Battista…'

Instantly, Misty understood what was making him tense and she was touched and pleased that he had decided to confide in her.

'Battista accepted a placement on Oliver Sargent's research staff last summer,' Leone advanced tight-mouthed. 'She was nineteen and she developed quite a crush on him.'

'Did she?' Misty looked surprised.

'He slept with her.'

Shocked by that statement, Misty frowned. 'Are you *sure* of that?'

'Certain. Her best friend was so distressed by her death that she told me the whole story. Sargent conducts his extra-marital affairs with great discretion. He owns a country cottage that only his lovers know exists.'

Misty lowered her attention from Leone's embittered gaze. So, the father who was a virtual stranger to her was *still* a womaniser, given to dishonesty and betrayal. No longer did she need to wonder what had caused the hostility between the two men, a hostility that Jenny Sargent had explained to her own satisfaction, ignorant as she had to be of the true facts.

'The night Battista died, she was driving Sargent down to his cottage, but I was unable to prove that he was in the car with her,' Leone admitted heavily. 'The car went off the road. There were no witnesses. She was trapped in the wreckage. He left her there and fled…'

Misty surveyed him in horror. 'Surely not?'

'It was well over an hour before an anonymous call was made to the emergency services. I very much doubt that he even risked making that call personally and, in any case, by then it was too late for Battista. My only consolation is that the medics told me that she couldn't have regained consciousness after the crash...' Leone's accented drawl had dropped low and roughened.

Misty was appalled at what he was telling her. 'How do you *know* that Oliver Sargent was with your sister?'

'I knew it the first time I saw him afterwards. I saw his guilt, his fear of exposure. He's a slick operator but he was terrified that I might be able to prove that he *was* with her that night. Unfortunately he has loyal friends willing to protect him.' His patent loathing for the man he blamed for his sister's death made Misty pale. 'One of those good friends let it be known that Oliver had spent that Friday evening driving down to Cornwall with him.'

'Have you ever confronted him?' she whispered sickly.

'He could sue me for making such an allegation without proof. His whole political career was riding on that alibi. I soon realised that, if I wanted to avenge Battista's death, I had to be even more devious than he is,' Leone admitted, lean, powerful face set in hard lines. 'Almost every public figure has something they want to conceal in their background. I had him investigated in great depth and that's how I found out about you...'

How I found out about you? That admission sent an alarm bell ringing in Misty's brain. She could see connections forming, the vague, horrendous outline of another dimension to their relationship that she could never have dreamt might exist. She sat there staring at him, willing him to tell her that her wild suspicions had no basis in fact.

'Oliver Sargent leads a double life. He's a corrupt politician and I wanted to expose him, but I also wanted him to suffer first.' Leone settled dark-as-midnight eyes on her waxen face. 'I chose you as my weapon.'

Misty parted bloodless lips. 'No…'

Leone sprang out of his seat and spread emphatic hands. 'I refused to see you as a person. I saw you purely as an extension of the man I hated beyond any other,' he told her with raw clarity. 'I had only the most cursory enquiries made about you and I was content to accept the rumours that you were far from being an angel. All that mattered to me was that your very *existence* was a threat to Oliver's reputation as the guardian of other people's morals.'

'Please tell me that this isn't true,' Misty mumbled in stricken appeal. 'Tell me I've woken up in a bad dream…'

'Nobody wants that miracle more than I do, *amore*,' Leone swore, studying her with fierce intensity. 'Do you think I *wanted* to tell you the truth? But I had no choice. Today you're in shock but by tomorrow you would've worked it all out for yourself. I hired you to pretend to be my mistress solely to get your face into the gossip columns and rouse the curiosity of the paparazzi…'

Leone was ten feet from her but that still felt too close. Sending her chair back in a sudden movement, Misty got up and backed away. A kind of fearful fascination held her attention to him, but really at that moment all she wanted to do was run and protect herself from hearing any more.

'I laid a trail so that the press could discover the link between you and Sargent for themselves. I intended you to meet him at Castle Eyrie,' Leone revealed with bitter regret. 'I changed my mind that same weekend because I saw what my revenge was likely to do to you. But by then it was too late to stop it…'

'Too late?' Misty questioned, her mind a bewildered

surge of incomplete thoughts, each one of which made her feel more betrayed than ever.

'I tried to prevent you from meeting Oliver because I knew that the moment he heard your name, he would realise who you were. I only went fishing to keep an eye on him but he got on the other boat and I lost track of him,' Leone reminded her, his strong jawline clenching hard. 'That same morning, while you were still asleep, I gave instructions that the evidence that linked you to Oliver Sargent should be buried again. But I had opened Pandora's box and I discovered I couldn't control what I had unleashed.'

Her legs were shaking beneath her and she sank down into an armchair. He had thrown too much at her at once for her to absorb it all immediately. Far from being his last option as a fake mistress, she had been his *only* option and hand-picked for the role. Sicilian business? Sicilian revenge. Her blood chilled in her veins. What kind of mind did it take for someone to use another human being as though they were an inanimate object of neither importance nor feeling? A very cold, calculating mind, she acknowledged, and the plan had been clever and callous in its very simplicity.

'No wonder you had to keep me in ignorance,' Misty condemned.

'Once I began to get to know you, I realised that what I was doing was wrong.'

But he had still got as far as taking her to Castle Eyrie to trail her in front of her father like a dumb fish lure there to hook a shark, so his regrets had only surfaced at the eleventh hour and only *after* he had slept with her. Up until that point she had simply been a thing, a cypher, a weapon and the very fact that he had paid her to take on that role of pretence must have made him feel even less compunction in using her to his own ends.

'Did you really think that money was likely to compensate me for what you've done to me?'

Leone released his breath in an audible rush. 'I'm ashamed to admit it…but at the beginning, yes, I did think that.'

'At least be honest!' Misty launched at him at sudden greater volume, colour beginning to fire over her cheekbones again. 'You didn't *care*.'

'I didn't want to consider that angle,' Leone countered doggedly.

With every minute that passed, she was grasping new realities. 'Was the idea of looking for a caterer to supply lunches for Brewsters all yours?'

Leone tensed. 'Yes.'

'And I got the contract because I was really the *only* applicant you wanted. It all went like clockwork, didn't it? Tell me, did you also hire a bunch of thugs to trash my business premises, knowing that I couldn't carry that loss and that Carlton Catering was that much more likely to go under?'

'Are you out of your mind?' Leone raked at her in angry, startled disbelief. 'I have no idea what you're talking about!'

'Just after I began that contract with Brewsters my premises were vandalised and my insurers refused to cover the damage.' Misty was impressed by the strength of his shaken rebuttal but impressed by nothing else, indeed far too deeply shaken to feel anything but alienation.

There was no more sobering or agonising discovery than the reality of learning that the man she had fallen in love with had been set on destroying her long before they had even exchanged a first kiss. He had planned her downfall, casting out the lure of that temporary contract and then sitting back to watch her take the bait and borrow on her prospects.

'You can't blame me for that misfortune or for the fact that you ran into financial trouble.' His dark golden eyes were grim on hers. 'But you can blame me for everything else that's happened to you!'

'Oh, don't worry,' Misty advised him unevenly. 'I'm blaming you, all right. But if my business hadn't got into trouble, how were you planning to persuade me to pretend to be your mistress?'

'I expected money to provide a sufficient persuasion.'

'And now I'm in debt to you to the tune of thousands and thousands of pounds and you are never going to see a penny of it back,' Misty swore between gritted teeth, striving to still the tremors of shock stealing through her taut, slender frame.

'I want nothing back. I rather hoped that we had moved beyond that point—'

'I don't think so. Before you went to New York, I asked you if I was still working for you and you said I *was*—'

Leone groaned out loud and flashed her a look of re-proof. 'If I'd told you that our agreement was history after our weekend in Scotland, you would have walked out on me out of pride,' he breathed rawly. 'I believed that I had dealt with the threat of the press exposing your relationship to Oliver Sargent. But I needed the time to establish a more normal relationship with you.'

'So you phoned me twice from New York…you're *so* attentive when you're keen, Leone.' Misty made that crack with her fingernails scoring welts into her palms.

His lean, strong face tensed. 'I was angry with you when I left.'

'After all that you have done, *you* were angry with *me*.'

'I care a lot about you. I didn't want to lose you.'

Misty dragged her pained gaze from the hard appeal in his and twisted her head away. 'You don't treat people you care about the way you've treated me. I could never forgive you for going to bed with me in the first place. Just because my supposed father had an affair with your sister…well, I'm sorry, but someone should have warned her not to mess around with a married man.'

There was a ghastly silence but she could not bring herself to look at him. She felt as if he had broken something precious inside her that she would never, ever be able to put together again. And maybe that something precious was faith, and she knew with a sinking heart that her own next step would be to blame herself for every wrong decision that she had made.

'Misty…'

'At that party at Castle Eyrie, Oliver Sargent came up to me. He told me not to trust you and to get out of your life because you were only using me,' Misty confided in a tight, flat little voice.

'You didn't tell me that…' Leone bit out in strong disconcertion.

'I thought he was drunk and that he just didn't like you.' A laugh empty of amusement fell from her lips. 'But now I'll always wonder if he felt sorry for me, if some tiny kernel of paternal concern motivated him. Yes, he no doubt wanted me to perform a vanishing act so that he could breathe easy again, but what *he* told me about you was the complete truth.'

As Misty completed that statement she watched Leone flinch as though she had struck him. A knock sounded on the door and, when it was ignored, sounded again. Opening the door, Leone spoke to the manservant and she turned her head away, feeling empty and despising herself for that last weak, wanton hour she had spent in his bedroom.

'Someone called Nancy has been trying to contact you at the apartment. She wants you to phone.'

In a split second, Misty had flown upright, galvanised by fear as she appreciated that Birdie might well have already received word of that dreadful newspaper article. 'Oh, *no*…'

Leone settled a phone into her hand and she punched out the numbers. But what Nancy had to tell her was entirely unexpected. Birdie had gone into hospital two days earlier, had the operation on her heart only the day before and had come through the surgery successfully.

Misty was stunned. 'But when was all that arranged?'

'We've had the date for a couple of weeks but Birdie wouldn't agree to tell you. She didn't want you to worry or come back from London on her behalf. She insisted I keep quiet about it until after the operation,' the older woman confided apologetically. 'I did *try* to reason with her but I was scared of upsetting her.'

Misty breathed in deep and slow, perspiration dampening her short upper lip. 'And she's *really* all right?'

Minutes later she set the phone down again, her mind grateful for the release of being able to concentrate on someone other than herself. In addition, while her thoughts had been stalled on what she was to do next out of sheer shock, her path was now simple and clear. She would go straight home and visit Birdie in hospital.

'What's happening?' Leone murmured tautly.

Misty refused to look at him. 'Birdie's had the heart surgery she was waiting on. I'm going home.'

The silence stretched.

'I'd very much like to meet your foster mother.'

'I can't think of one reason why she would want to meet you.'

Momentarily silenced by that reroute, Leone said flatly, 'A limo will take you back.'

A limo would get her there faster than the train, Misty reflected. She walked out into the hall as if he weren't there and, in many ways at that moment, Leone *was* no longer real to her. The guy she had fallen madly in love

with had evaporated before her eyes and she did not want
to take account of a replacement who was chilling, callous
and cruel.

'Give me the chance to make this up to you,' Leone
ground out a split second before she departed from his
house again.

With a frown of disbelief, Misty looked up at him and
encountered fierce dark golden eyes, recognising the extent
of the tension holding him still. 'But you *couldn't*,' she
whispered. 'You scare the living daylights out of me...'

All the way back to Fossetts the expression on his darkly
handsome face stayed in her mind's eye. He had looked
so shocked. But what had he expected? At the end of the
day, she had been faced with the hard reality that she had
allowed her heart and her body to overrule all intelligence
and common sense. What had she been doing, getting involved with a ruthless Sicilian tycoon? Hadn't she been
well aware of his reputation even before she'd tangled with
him? At what stage had she begun convincing herself that
he was a real pussycat beneath the tough front? Warm and
affectionate and caring? My goodness, there was no end
to the things a woman in love could make herself believe...

Three weeks later, Misty sat in the waiting room in the
local doctor's surgery.

Birdie had been released from hospital the week before
but her foster mother had opted to spend her convalescence
in Oxford with her sister, who had recently lost her husband. While scolding herself for being so selfish, Misty
had been really disappointed that Birdie hadn't been coming home to Fossetts immediately.

Right at that moment, she was wondering why the doctor had asked her to wait for the test results. She was only
feeling a bit off colour and she had been frank with him.

She had told him that she had had a recent major emotional upset and that her nervous stomach dated from that same day, and she had advised him to check her notes when he had asked her if she could be pregnant. Everything was Leone's fault: her misery, her dippy digestion, her vanished menstrual cycle, her newfound ability to go off into tears over the stupidest things.

Leone had phoned her and she had put the phone down on him. When he had not called back, she'd told herself that she was grateful that he had taken the hint. However, a week after that, she had been furious to learn that Leone had visited Birdie in hospital. Birdie had pronounced him charming and had got on like a house on fire with him. But then Birdie had not the slightest idea of what had happened between Leone and her foster daughter.

Misty could not understand how being without Leone could feel as if someone had stolen the sun from her world. After all, she had lived a long time without him and had known him for only a matter of months. Yet no matter how often she reminded herself that he had used her with ruthless disregard of the damage he might be inflicting, her sense of loss, emptiness and dislocation merely deepened with every passing day.

'Miss Carlton…' The receptionist indicated that she could go back in to see the doctor.

'Three years ago, you were warned that you might only conceive with the help of fertility treatment, but doctors tend to be very cautious when the prognosis is uncertain,' Dr Fleming told her gravely. 'Evidently you recovered well from the surgery that you had then because you *have* conceived.'

Barely having had the chance to sit down, Misty blinked. 'Sorry?'

'You're going to have a baby.'

She kept on staring at the older man, unable to absorb

the immensity of that announcement. At first, it felt like a cruel joke and she couldn't credit it, and then this great surge of hope swept through her and left her head swimming.

'Now, as I gather that this is an unplanned event...' he continued ruefully.

'It's not an unplanned event...it's a miracle,' Misty contradicted simply.

Fifteen minutes later, having listened unconvinced to the doctor telling her that he did not think her pregnancy lay within the realms of a miracle, Misty floated out of the surgery and straight down the main street into the nearest baby shop. She looked at the tiny clothes with reverent eyes, roved over to admire the buggies, and went off into a wonderful daydream over the soft toys.

Leone had got her pregnant. He had broken her heart, but what was a heart with a crack set next to a baby? A little boy, a little girl. She had no preference whatsoever. She bought a book on pregnancy. Leone's baby. She pushed out that thought as soon as it popped up. This was *her* baby. It was nothing to do with Leone. At least he had made himself useful in one direction, she reflected with a distinct sense of one-upmanship.

She noticed the board outside a newsagent's advertising the morning papers' biggest headline: SARGENT RESIGNS... It was not a surprise. In recent weeks, Oliver Sargent had rarely been out of the newspapers. Within days of Misty's existence being revealed, more serious allegations had been lodged against the older man: that he had accepted bribes in the form of expensive gifts and favours from dubious businessmen in return for using his influence on their behalf. As the evidence of his wrongdoing had mounted, his keen defenders had fallen silent and the ruin of his political career had seemed inevitable.

Momentarily, Misty felt sorry for the father she had

never known, but it was hard to care that much about a man who had made no attempt to contact her. Yet, apart from her twin and herself, he had no other children. Did he blame her for precipitating his downfall? Or was he just as uninterested in her now as he had been in her at birth? And did she even *want* contact with the man whom Leone believed had left his kid sister lying injured in a car wreck just to protect himself from scandal?

On the drive back to Fossetts, Misty thought about Carlton Catering and grimaced. During her absence, two of her three staff had found other employment. Although Misty had initially been delighted to be hired for several private dinner parties, her belief that her business was back up and running had been shortlived. She had suffered the excruciating embarrassment of being made to feel like a freak show by clients, who it seemed had largely sought her services so that they could tell their guests that she was Oliver Sargent's illegitimate daughter and the cast-off mistress of a Sicilian tycoon.

Now that she knew that she was pregnant, selling her business and just finding a job seemed a better option. Furthermore, with the proceeds of the sale, she could start repaying the money she had accepted from Leone before she'd realised that he had hired her to destroy her own father. She knew she would not be able to live with herself until she had begun settling that debt.

In the sitting room at Fossetts, Misty sat down to deal with the morning post. She was disconcerted to open a letter from the company that held the mortgage that contained a cheque written out to the exact amount of her last payment. Getting on the phone to ask why that payment had been refunded, she was astonished to be told that the mortgage had been settled in full prior to the arrival of her cheque.

Silenced by that shock announcement, she replaced the

receiver, instantly aware that only Leone could have made such an extravagant gesture. Sheer rage hurtled through her taut frame. So Leone still believed that he could buy her, did he? Well, she would soon disabuse him of that notion. She wanted nothing to do with him and no more of his wretched money either. As it was, she was likely to be paying him off for the rest of her days! Determined to confront him on the issue, she changed into a red stretchy dress that always made her feel feisty and she tidied her hair. Just as she was telling Nancy that she was going down to London, the doorbell went.

'Where's my red carpet?' Flash demanded, standing back to strike an attitude, spiky blond hair catching the sunlight, green eyes enjoying the effect he was having on her. Behind his metallic gold customised sports car a carload of minders built like human tanks were climbing out of their vehicle.

It had been five months since Misty had seen him, two since she had spoken to him on the phone. For a split second she hesitated, and then she threw herself into his open arms, eyes stinging with tears. He held her back from him and his keen gaze hardened. 'Why do you always pick bastards?'

'S-sorry?' she stammered as he walked her into the sitting room with the familiarity of a male who had often stayed at Fossetts.

'I may have been touring the US but I still follow the English papers,' Flash said very drily. 'You never called me once. Yet it's been all thrills and spills here. One minute you're swanking round in diamonds with this Mafioso type, the next you're discovering you have the long-lost daddy from hell…a politician…how low can you sink? And then you get dumped.'

Misty's chin came up. 'Excuse me? I dumped him.'

Resting back against the table, his lanky, compact length

complemented by a black T-shirt and faded jeans, Flash gave her a huge approving smile. 'That makes me feel a lot better. Where's Birdie?'

While she was explaining, Flash, who was rarely still for longer than ten seconds, picked up the fat paperback still lying on the table and grimaced. 'Who's reading this?'

Misty turned scarlet. It was the pregnancy book she had bought.

'What are you reading stuff like that for? You're only upsetting yourself!' Flash groaned with a look of incomprehension. 'I thought you'd got over that.'

She almost let his assumption stand and then guilt kicked in and she told him the truth. In shock, he closed his eyes and swore long and low under his breath.

'Something good has come out of something bad,' Misty muttered fiercely.

'It's a bloody disaster!' Flash launched at her angrily.

An hour later, he knew everything, right down to the fact that when he'd arrived she had been on the brink of heading out to catch a train down to London.

'So I'll take you instead,' Flash stunned her by announcing, an air of grim pleasure lightening his eyes at the prospect. 'And after you've told the Mafioso what he can do with himself, we'll go out and celebrate!'

Ten minutes later, an overnight bag hastily filled, she was in the car and it was roaring down the drive.

CHAPTER NINE

FLASH had not the smallest difficulty talking his way into the underground car park at Andracchi Industries.

When Misty arrived on the top floor, the receptionist called Leone's secretary with her name. With her mane of copper hair and the red dress that enhanced her lithe, shapely figure, she was attracting an uncomfortable amount of attention by then and her nerves were eating her alive. When Leone strode into view in person, a breath-taking smile on his lean, dark features, her mouth ran dry and her heart started beating like a war drum. After three weeks of cold turkey withdrawal symptoms and the kind of dreams that made her despise herself in the morning light, his stunning dark good looks and lean, well-built physique had a powerfully embarrassing effect on her.

Angrily ashamed of the leap of response attacking her treacherous body, Misty parted her lips and without even pausing for breath snapped, 'How *dare* you pay off Birdie's mortgage?'

Brilliant golden eyes shimmered over her from head to toe and he took his time over that appraisal before resting his attention back on her furious face. 'We'll go into my office.'

'What I have to say can be said right here!'

'But if you expect me to *listen*, you don't begin by abusing me in a reception area,' Leone murmured with icy cool.

Recalled to an awareness of their surroundings and genuinely mortified by her own thoughtless behaviour, Misty reddened to the roots of her hair and accompanied him down a corridor into an impressive office.

She stole a covert glance at him as he closed the door, taking in his bold, bronzed profile, the sleek, sophisticated cut of his suit and the slice of pristine white shirt-cuff visible above a lean, long-fingered hand. As a tide of aching regret charged her she swallowed hard. His every movement was measured and fluid and oh, so cool and she was intimidated by his apparent detachment. He offered her a seat but she declined.

'Can I abuse you now?' Misty enquired.

'I wouldn't advise it, *amore*.' Leone held eye contact far longer than was comfortable for her strained nerves.

'Don't call me that.'

'As far as I'm concerned, you're still my lover until I take another,' Leone imparted smooth as silk.

Another? That one word threatened to slice Misty in two. The very idea of him with another woman devastated her, froze her brain in its tracks and sent her heart swooping to her toes. Her fingers curled in on themselves as she willed herself back under control, but it took every atom of pride that she possessed.

'I'll ask you again.' Misty lifted her chin. 'What were you playing at when you settled Birdie's mortgage?'

A wry smile curved Leone's wide sensual mouth. 'I'm afraid you're out of bounds.'

Her temper began to rise again. 'I beg your pardon?'

'You heard me.'

'But I know *exactly* why you did it!' Misty condemned.

'Do you?' Leone surveyed her with veiled golden eyes that gleamed like the purest metal.

'Of course I blasted well know!' Misty fired back at him in furious frustration, unable to fathom his attitude. 'You're trying to impress me with your generosity and get me back—'

'No, I'm not.'

But Misty had worked up too big a head of steam to pay proper heed to that quiet contradiction. 'You think you can persuade me that you're really a nice person...you think you can *bribe* me back into your bed with the power of your money—'

'No, I don't.'

'And it's disgusting and what's more...a total waste of your time...' As Misty finally took in Leone's denials her voice faded away instead of reaching a crescendo. Silenced, she stared at him in visible confusion.

'I don't owe you an explanation but, since you've mis-understood the gesture, I'll tell you what motivated me,' Leone murmured evenly. 'In the guise of an anonymous well-wisher, I settled your foster mother's mortgage be-cause I liked her.'

'Because you liked her...' Misty echoed weakly.

'I give millions to charity every year. I have no hands-on involvement.' Leone informed her. 'But when I met Birdie, I found myself wondering how often deserving in-dividuals like her are passed over as being not sufficiently deprived to require help. Yet she and her husband, at no little cost to themselves, devoted their lives to working with troubled children.'

'Yes, that's true *but*—'

'If Robin Pearce hadn't quit his career as an award-winning architect forty years ago, his widow would've been left comfortably off. At this stage of her life, Birdie should not have to pay a price for their generosity towards others.' His strong jawline clenched. 'In short, if I choose to play Santa Claus, it's my money and my choice.'

The silence sizzled with as much danger as bare electric wires.

Misty was pale as death, for she could see that he meant every word that he had just said. And she wanted to sink through the floor. She wanted to shrivel into invisibility, anything sooner than be forced to bear the awful humiliation she had brought down on her own head. She had screeched at him like a shrew. She had accused him of going to extraordinary lengths to get her back. She must have sounded so vain, so self-absorbed, so far removed from reality. Even after soundly rejecting him, she had somehow contrived to go on believing that he remained interested in her.

'As I suspect that you virtually beggared yourself to keep your foster mother in that house,' Leone continued, 'you should be relieved.'

To Misty's horror tears stung her eyes in a hot surge and she spun away in panic, only to stagger as a blinding wave of dizziness engulfed her. Strong arms steadied her as she swayed and he backed her down into a seat.

'What have you been doing to yourself?' Leone demanded with audible concern.

As she sucked in extra oxygen to clear her head, the trickle of tears threatened to become a gush capable of washing him right out of his office again. Determined to hold all that moisture in, she bent her head and the dreadful silence stretched.

'Why did you come all the way down here to see me?' Leone breathed huskily.

'Rage.' Misty lifted her lashes and almost had a heart attack. Having dropped down into an atheletic crouch, he was right in front of her and only inches away.

'Start shouting again. At this moment, all I want to do is drag you down onto the carpet and lose myself in you again,' Leone confided thickly.

Misty collided with smouldering golden eyes and her heart skipped a beat.

His arrogant head angled to one side, he devoured her

with his molten gaze and then murmured, 'That's fantasy... I'd be more than happy to settle for dinner.'

She was appalled to realise that the reference to the carpet and sexual activity combined with him still had extraordinary appeal. At the speed of light she had gone from sick dizziness to burning, wanton lust and the most agonised craving. Soft, full mouth taut, she stared at him as though he had her imprisoned behind steel bars. Her brain was telling her to stand up and walk out, but her body was glued to the seat and shamefully hot and liquid with longing. At violent war with her own instincts, she trembled.

'No...I can't.' Desperate to think of anything but his proximity and her own weak reaction to him, Misty made herself concentrate on his benevolence towards Birdie. Like it or not, she too would benefit from that altruistic gesture, but at least it meant that she could immediately return a good deal of the cash he had advanced to her after that contract had been signed. Removing her cheque-book from her bag, she balanced it on her knee and began to fill out a cheque.

Leone frowned. 'What are you doing?'

Misty handed the cheque to him.

He quirked an ebony brow and vaulted back upright. 'What's this for?'

Her triangular face set and her eyes veiled, she stood up. 'It's the first payment on what I owe you,' she said stiffly. 'Primarily, I took your money to keep up the payments on Birdie's mortgage but you've taken care of that problem for me.'

His strong jawline had clenched. 'I told you that I wanted nothing back.'

'I didn't want to be involved in my father's downfall...unfortunately you didn't give me a choice about that. However, I *can* refuse to profit from his misfortunes,' Misty declared, her bright head high, but her heart twisting inside her as she saw the flare of angry reproach in his gaze.

She could imagine only too well how agonising it must have been for Leone when his kid sister had died in such appalling circumstances, and how embittered he must have been when he'd realised that Oliver Sargent could not be called to account through the normal legal channels. But two wrongs did not make a right and his ferocious need for revenge had hurt her a great deal, as well as highlighting the awful truth that there was no way on earth Leone could *ever* have a normal relationship with the daughter of a man whom he hated.

In the simmering silence, Leone tore the cheque in two.

Her legs feeling like hollow wood, Misty kept moving towards the door and opened it. 'I'll donate the money to charity, then.'

'You can't afford to do that either!' Leone dismissed in exasperation.

'I'm selling my business. If it doesn't find a buyer as a going concern, I'll sell off the equipment and the vans.'

Leone surveyed her with savage incredulity. 'Are you out of your mind?'

A bitter smile curved Misty's soft mouth as she allowed herself a final word. 'Thanks to all that publicity, I've acquired a certain notoriety locally. Listening from the kitchen while my clients and their guests discuss me is not my idea of fun.'

A line of hard colour scored his superb cheekbones and she knew she need say nothing more, for his pride was as strong as her own.

She hurried on down the corridor, her back rigid and her throat convulsing. Before the lift doors could shut she surged in and hit the button for the basement floor. Secure in the belief that she was alone, she rested her hot, damp forehead against the cold steel wall, just as the doors jerked back again and someone else stepped in. Flushed and dis-comfited, she turned round to find herself facing Leone again.

His smouldering golden gaze held hers in the pulsing silence. Her shoulder blades met the wall behind her, but the throb of awareness surged through her in an electrical storm of sensation. When he reached for her, she was breathing fast and audibly and the frantic ache stirring within her had no conscience. All that mattered in that instant was the hot, potent explosion of his sensual mouth on hers, the hard, satisfying strength of his hands as he plastered her up against every muscular angle of his lean, powerful frame. She was welded to him when the loud ping of the lift's arrival penetrated the fog of her excite-ment and she jerked back from him in dismay.

Her dazed attention fell on the car parked only about thirty feet away. The driver's door was already opening, a blond head appearing.

'I've got to go...Flash is waiting,' she muttered in a rush.

But as she made it out of the lift Leone closed his hand over hers to halt her. 'What are you doing with *him*?' he demanded with savage abruptness.

Misty tried and failed to pull away. 'That's none of your business—'

'Let go of her!' Flash demanded, striding towards them, his anger unconcealed.

In the background, Misty saw Flash's minders leaping out of their vehicle, scenting trouble and, by the expression on their tough faces, looking forward to the prospect. Every alarm bell she possessed started clanging. Leone against three men. Spinning round to face him, she gasped, 'Get back in the lift, you idiot!'

In a slow, emphatic movement, Leone released her. 'Stay out of this—'

Misty simply stepped in front of him. 'If you touch him, I'll never forgive you!' she flung at Flash in a passion. 'I don't want trouble and I won't have *stupid* male hormones taking over here!'

'I'm not about to stand by watching him manhandle a pregnant woman!' Flash growled at her. 'And stop embarrassing us. He's a big guy. He can look after himself.'

The angry colour in Misty's cheeks drained away long before the younger man finished speaking. Appalled by his reference to the child she was carrying and hearing Leone vent his breath in a startled hiss behind her, Misty gave her foster brother a stricken look.

'You're pregnant?' Leone exclaimed in disbelief.

Misty closed her hand round Flash's wrist and tried to drag him in the direction of the car. 'Come on…' she urged.

'Is it mine?' Leone muttered hoarsely.

And Flash swung round and went for him. It happened so fast, she had no hope of preventing that outbreak of aggression. She was just in time to see Leone duck and plant a punch on Flash instead.

'Stop it…stop it, the two of you!' she shrieked, her voice breaking with the force of her distress.

Ironically, Leone stilled just long enough to allow Flash the opportunity to return that punch.

At that point, registering that Flash's minders were staying out of the fray and no longer caring if the two men killed each other, Misty threw herself into the passenger seat of the car. *Is it mine?* She felt savaged. How could Leone have asked such a question?

Minutes later, Flash settled with a groan in beside her. 'Honour's been satisfied,' he informed her.

Misty stared out through the windscreen. Still as a statue, Leone was poised by the lift watching them, lean, strong features grim and set.

'You're supposed to thank me for defending your honour,' Flash told her. 'How was I supposed to know you hadn't told him about the baby? I mean…I assumed that was one of the *main* reasons you wanted to see him—'

'I only found out that I was pregnant this morning. I hadn't even thought about telling Leone yet,' Misty admitted tightly. 'And after what he said, I'm glad I didn't bother.'

'I wouldn't make too much out of Andracchi asking whose baby it was.' Flash grimaced. 'You were with me and he didn't like it…and me knowing what he *didn't* know would have made any bloke suspicious.'

'My goodness, you're really quite in charity with Leone now that you've thumped each other!' Misty responded with waspish bite.

'What are you planning to tell Birdie?'

Misty jerked and paled, for that was a challenge she had avoided even thinking about.

'She'll be devastated—' Flash forecast ruefully.

'Yes, I do *know* that!' Misty interrupted on the back of a guilty sob, knowing that Birdie would be shocked, hurt and very disappointed in her. Indeed, the older woman would very likely blame herself for some perceived and quite imaginary flaw in her own parenting skills.

'So, taking everything into account, I'm just amazed that you were carrying on in that lift with Andracchi!'

Her cheeks burning, Misty looked at her foster brother.

Flash cast her a mocking glance. 'You left lipstick on him.'

He took her back to his city apartment, ordered in a take-away for his entire entourage and sat down with them to watch the football matches taped for him while he'd been out of the country. Exhausted by her eventful day, refusing to think about Leone's forbidding reaction to the news that she was carrying his child, Misty fell asleep on a sofa. Flash woke her up several hours later to tell her to get ready to go out. It was already late and Misty was not in the mood, but, feeling guilty about being such a wet blanket, she washed her hair and made a special effort to look her most festive in the emerald-green and cerise top and hipster skirt she had packed.

A bank of cameras greeted Flash's arrival at his favourite London nightclub and she kept a bright smile pinned to her peach tinted mouth. If a photo made it into print and Leone saw it, she wanted to look as though she hadn't a care in the world.

Seated by the management at a reserved table, Flash closed an appreciative arm around her. 'You never complained once about the football—'

Misty grinned. '*Only* because I slept through it.'

'I've missed you, but you could be bad for my image,' Flash said with amusement. 'You tower over me like a Vegas showgirl!'

People kept coming up to talk to him. It was the early hours of the morning when Misty saw Leone through the crush. He was watching their table, lean, powerful face hard as iron. Her heart thumped, butterflies breaking loose in her tummy. Keen not to draw Flash's attention to him and knowing that she had to talk to Leone, she slid out from behind the table. But no sooner did she reach him than he simply closed one imprisoning hand over hers and began to press her towards the exit.

'What are you doing?' she gasped, but the music was too loud for him to hear her.

In the foyer, Misty rounded on him. 'I can't just walk out of here!'

'It's almost dawn and you're out dancing and drinking with another guy!' Sizzling golden eyes flared over her in furious derision. 'You're coming home with me—'

'No, I'm not, and the only thing I've been drinking is

pineapple juice!' Misty hissed back at him, wholly disconcerted by that attack.

Ignoring that plea, Leone turned to speak to one of the security men, and beneath her shaken gaze money changed hands faster than the speed of light. Leone curved a hand round the base of her rigid spine. 'Your pet rock star will get a message...OK?'

'No. I came here with Flash and I'll leave with him.'

Leone resting blazing golden eyes on her. 'You have two options, *amore*. Either you accompany me of your own accord *or*...I carry you out of here.'

Misty looked at him aghast. Already conscious that speculative eyes were resting on them, she reddened with angry incredulity. 'You wouldn't dare...'

'Wouldn't I?' Leone countered lethally. 'I've been trying to track you down since yesterday. Almost twelve hours on, I wouldn't say that my patience is at an all time high.'

At his admission that he had been looking for her ever since she had left the scene of that stupid fight, Misty worried at the soft underside of her lip and then walked out of the nightclub without further protest. Of course he wanted to speak to her after what he had found out. Was she afraid of what she was about to hear? Trying to avoid the unpleasantness? Naturally he had been shocked and angry the day before. What had been a casual sexual fling on his terms had had far-reaching consequences. He had asked her if it had been safe to make love and she had told him it had been, but she was now carrying his baby. She would be a fool to hope that from his point of view that could be anything other than very bad news.

Leone unlocked the door of a low-slung red sports car. She climbed in. He drove off and still the silence was maintained, worrying at her nerves, keeping her tension high.

'I'd like to know how you feel about this baby,' Leone confessed at the first set of traffic lights.

Fearing that he was asking that because he was hoping that she might be willing to consider a termination, she realised that she had to be totally honest. 'I'm sure you don't want to hear it…but I was over the moon when I found out,' she admitted tautly. 'I thought I couldn't have a child and to me it just feels like a miracle. But I don't expect anyone else to feel the same way. I know the circumstances are hardly ideal.'

Leone was listening with such intensity that the lights changed without him noticing and only the angry revving of the car behind recalled him to that reality. His masculine profile a little less taut, he drove on. She looked at his lean brown fingers where they rested on the steering wheel and felt her skin heat as she remembered the way he made love. Her colour heightening at what seemed the ultimate of inappropriate memories, she turned her head away.

'I had a surprise visitor shortly after your departure yesterday,' Leone breathed tautly. 'Oliver Sargent—'

Misty emerged from her self-absorption with a start. 'He came to see you? But *why*?'

'He finally confessed that he *was* with Battista the night she died. According to him he threw himself out of the car as it went off the road and he was knocked out. He said that Battista was dead by the time he recovered consciousness and that he panicked.'

'Do you believe him?' Misty whispered.

'Yes,' Leone ceded in a roughened undertone. 'By admitting that he had lied to the police when he was initially approached about the crash, he put himself in my power.'

'And are you planning to inform the police?'

'What good would that serve now?'

A shaken little laugh escaped Misty. 'So, really, it was *all* for nothing.'

'No. I got the truth and I don't regret helping the press to expose his corrupt practices in government. I only regret the harm I caused you,' Leone completed without hesitation.

She was disconcerted by the extent of her own relief at learning that her father had not left Leone's sister lying injured and alone. She could well imagine the older man's panic and fear of exposure in the aftermath of that accident and, although she could not condone his lies, she was pleased that he had had the courage and the decency to finally tell Leone what had really happened that night.

It was a surprise when Leone took her to the apartment where she had lived so briefly. As she walked into the hall he murmured in evident explanation, 'You left clothes here.'

He meant the wardrobe that he had bought her, not one item of which had she taken home with her. 'Yes…'

Misty sat down on a sofa, stiff with unease and a sense of being under imminent attack. Left to herself, she reflected, she might never have told him about the baby, reasoning that at least that way she retained her dignity and her pride.

Leone studied her from beneath black spiky lashes, stunning eyes intent. 'I want us to get married.'

'S-sorry?' Misty stammered, her silvery eyes widening in shock and her lips parted.

'No, don't start arguing with me. Hear me out first,' Leone said levelly. 'This is my baby too. I'd like my child to have my name and the same love and security that my father gave me.'

Unable to stay still, Misty stood up on legs that felt wobbly and stared at him, reading the gravity in his lean, darkly handsome features. Initially she was so shaken by that proposal that she could think of nothing to say. It was the very last response that she had expected from him.

'Sicilians have a very strong sense of family,' Leone asserted, his strong jawline clenching. 'You know that to your cost already, but there is a brighter side to the equation.'

'Is there?' Walking over to the tall windows with barely a sense of where she was going or what she was doing, never mind what she was saying, Misty could not drag her eyes from him.

'Do you want to be a single parent like your own mother?'

Instantly, Misty bristled. 'Don't bring my background into this. I could manage on my own—'

'But you don't have to manage alone. Don't punish our child for *my* sins,' Leone cut in with hard emphasis.

That warning shook Misty. Had she been trying to punish him? She had assumed that he would have little interest in a baby that had been conceived without his wish or agreement, for that had been true of her own father and equally true for many of the other foster children with whom she had grown up. She had also believed that only mothers had feelings and loyalties towards an unborn child and he had just proven her wrong.

'I wasn't expecting this,' she confessed unevenly, her hands closing together and then parting again. 'I mean…do you honestly think you could stick with a marriage over the head of a baby you didn't plan for?'

Flags of pink ran up into Misty's cheeks as she realised how revealing her own question had been. She had just betrayed the fact that she was considering his offer and computing the chances of him staying the distance as a husband.

'I want you back in my bed too, *amore*.' Leone held her startled upward glance with a frank and earthy intensity that made her breath catch in her throat and shame-faced heat surge at the very heart of her body. 'Marriages have survived on a lot less.'

She could have drummed up a dozen sensible reasons for marrying Leone. She knew exactly how difficult it was to be a single parent with nobody else to fall back on for support. Furthermore, if she married Leone, she would not have to worry about making ends meet or educating her child in the future. And last and not least their baby would benefit in many ways from having a father who cared.

But Misty was ashamed to acknowledge that not one of those worthy arguments would have made much impression on her had she not been in love with Leone. That was the crux of the matter. By stressing the needs of their child, he had given her a face-saving excuse to bring him back into her life and, much as she despised her own weakness, she knew that she was about to snatch at that excuse.

'OK…' Misty could not bring herself to look at Leone as she voiced that casual agreement lest he recognise the sudden intense spasm of relief assailing her at the realisation that she would be able to stop fighting herself every hour of every day. For that was what getting by without Leone had meant: a constant inner battle against her own weak-willed impulses and needs.

The silence lay heavy and she was tempted into glancing across the room. Leone was surveying her with narrowed dark eyes as though she had surprised him.

'I'm thinking of what's best for the baby,' Misty heard herself say as if she were a sacrificial lamb.

'Why not?' Leone countered, smooth as silk. 'If it wasn't for the baby, we wouldn't be having this conversation.'

Her fingers curled into momentary talons and then bit into her palms. She would have liked to unleash a stinging retaliation but he had voiced a humiliating and unarguable truth.

'We'll apply for a licence, so that we can have the wedding as soon as possible,' Leone continued.

Misty nodded, the delicate lines of her face icily composed.

'Would you like another pineapple juice to celebrate?'

'No, thanks. I'd like to go to bed now, if that's all right with you.' Pride prevented Misty from making any move towards him because she was determined not to reveal how strong her own feelings were for him. Yet she knew that her own assurance that she was marrying him solely for the baby's benefit had been ungenerous and cold. But she still very much wanted the coolness that had opened up between them to be bridged and took her time about leaving the room in the hope that he would say or do something to prevent her.

But Leone did nothing. As she glanced back over her shoulder she saw him by the window, strain etched in his hard male profile, savage tension emanating from the set of his powerful shoulders, and her throat thickened with tears.

He had shown neither censure nor resentment in a situation that would have tried most men. He had accepted responsibility for their child and he had asked her to marry him. But that did not mean that *he* was any happier than *she* was, for he knew and she knew that she was still blaming him for the manner in which he had used her to gain revenge on her father.

Yet he had acknowledged his mistake and tried not only to prevent her from coming into contact with her father that weekend at Castle Eyrie, but had also attempted to put a lid on the ensuing press revelations. That he had failed might be his own fault too for ever embarking on such a ruthless scheme, but was she planning to hold that against him for ever?

She lay in bed examining her own flaws: she was not

very good at forgiving those who hurt her. She had been hurt too often as a child and she had learned then to withdraw into a harder shell and to fight back to protect herself. She knew that Leone felt guilty and that guilt was destructive. Did she really want their marriage to suffer from that added burden?

She loved him so much it terrified her and maybe refusing to forgive him was easier than dealing with the reality that he did *not* love her, she acknowledged painfully. But had she been a little braver and a lot less proud, she would not be lying alone and miserable in bed aching for him with every fibre of her being…

In sudden rebellion, Misty slid out of bed, padded down the corridor and walked into Leone's bedroom before she could lose her nerve. Just as she entered he emerged from the bathroom stark naked and towelling his hair dry, six feet four inches of lithe, powerful masculinity. His stunning golden eyes locked to her and he let the towel fall as he strode forward.

A feverish flush colouring her face, she read the smouldering invitation in his raking scrutiny. Her heart pounded as he reached for her, tugging her up against his hard, muscular length and murmuring with roughened satisfaction, '*Dio mio, amore*…you always have the power to surprise me.'

She had surprised herself almost as much, only now thought was being overwhelmed by her own response. Her breasts were full and straining below the fine satin nightgown, tender peaks taut with arousal, and a dulled throb pulsed low in her pelvis. Weak with anticipation, she shivered, shocked by her own hunger. He picked her up and laid her down on the bed and peeled her out of the nightdress.

Leone released his breath in a sexy sound of appreciation. 'I'm so hot for you, I hardly know where to begin…'

He bent his dark head to encircle a rosy peak with the tip of his tongue and a low sighing moan escaped her as reaction shot right to the fiery heart of her. She closed her hands over his wide, muscular shoulders, loving the smoothness of his skin there, the masculine heat and scent of him, spreading her restive fingers in sensual pleasure.

'Kiss me...' she urged, letting her hands close into his damp black hair.

That long, drugging collision of their mouths left her quivering and hotter than ever. His fingertips teased through the nest of downy curls crowning her femininity and she arched up her hips and parted her thighs, wild excitement charging her as he discovered the slick wet heat of her.

'You drive me crazy with desire, *amore*,' Leone growled, rising over her in one powerful movement and sinking slow and deep into her.

She sobbed out loud with the wild, fierce pleasure of his invasion. All the seething emotional turmoil of the past twenty-four hours was finding an outlet in passion. She moved against him, all writhing heat and abandonment, letting the great swell of excitement snatch her up and control her until it flung her higher than she had ever reached before in a white hot blinding surge of fulfilment.

In the aftermath, she still felt as though she were floating and as Leone shifted back from her she leant over him, silver-grey eyes bright with emotion, and whispered, 'I died and went to heaven the day I found you.'

A wolfish grin of appreciation slashed his wide, sensual mouth. 'Are you sure you're feeling all right? You don't sound at all like yourself.'

'Enjoy it while it lasts,' she advised, happiness flooding through her as he curved her close and pressed a slow, sweet kiss to her reddened mouth.

'I didn't realise I'd found heaven until I stumbled into hell,' Leone traded feelingly.

She caught sight of her watch and tensed with guilt as she recalled the way in which she had left that club a couple of hours earlier. 'Flash is going to be *very* annoyed with me—'

His big, powerful frame tensed beneath hers. 'You don't need him. You have me—'

Misty laughed. 'I plan to hang onto both of you.'

'No.' Hauling himself up against the pillows, a virile vision of bronzed skin and rippling muscles, Leone studied her with hard dark eyes. 'I want him out of your life.'

'Well, what you want isn't always what you get,' Misty informed him gently.

'You ran to him when Redding dumped you three years ago…and you ran to him this time too—'

'You didn't dump me…I dumped *you*!' Misty heard herself launch at him full volume, temper roused by that unnecessary reference to her former fiancé.

'I'll treat that comment with the contempt it deserves.' Stunningly handsome dark features taut with anger, Leone threw back the sheets and sprang out of bed. 'I've seen how you behave with Flash.'

Taking that as an incendiary reference to her most embarrassing moment, Misty went rigid. 'I doubt very much that I'll be tempted to get up on a stage at our wedding and dance!'

'*Santo Cielo*! I'm talking about what I saw only *two* hours ago! He had his arms round you—'

'Flash is a very touchy-feely person and so am I—

'Not with me,' Leone slotted in between gritted white teeth.

Misty thought about that and it was quite true, but then she was in love with Leone and always on her guard around him. It was a case of…when he got affectionate with her outside the bedroom door, she would get affectionate with him. 'I don't think that's relevant. I'm very fond of Flash but we *are* only friends—'

'He has a lousy reputation with women—'

'He's only twenty-four…and, really, where *you* get the nerve to criticise *him* for that, I honestly don't know!' Misty exclaimed.

'If you're going to be my wife, you need to learn to listen to my point of view.'

That measured intonation sent a chill running through Misty and she paled. She dropped her eyes, wondering how they could be at daggers drawn when only minutes ago they had been in each other's arms. It was ironic that the crises in her own life had allowed her and Flash to rediscover their friendship over the past twenty-four hours. But possibly she was being unreasonable to expect Leone to forgive and forget the reality that he and Flash had been exchanging punches the day before.

'You'll be so busy planning our wedding that you won't have time to worry about anything else,' Leone informed her in bracing addition.

As she listened to the shower running. Misty slid back into her nightdress. Did Leone think she was a silly little girl he could distract with platitudes? She had no intention of severing her ties with Flash. Very tempted to ask Leone if his definition of a wife dated back to the old dark days of female servitude, she decided it would be wiser to return to her own bedroom.

Indeed, only when she got back into her bed did comprehension sink in on her. Leone was jealous. Why hadn't she recognised that? He was jealous of her close friendship with Flash. Recalling the manner in which he had reacted to Philip right at the start of their relationship, she started to smile. Leone was complex but very straightforward in some ways. He wasn't at all sure of her either. The more she thought about that, the more she loved him, for she had finally found a chink in his rock-solid self-assurance.

CHAPTER TEN

A WEEK later, Misty was dreamily removing her wedding gown from its packaging when Birdie called up the stairs to her.

'You have a visitor, Misty!'

In less than twenty-four hours she would be Leone's wife, and she was viewing their impending marriage along the lines of a campaign in which she would make herself so irresistible that Leone would fall for her like a ton of bricks. By the time she had finished with him, he really wasn't going to know what had hit him. She could plot and plan too, couldn't she?

The wedding arrangements had been made at the speed of light. No sooner had she phoned Birdie in Oxford to inform her of what was afoot than Birdie had persuaded her widowed sister to return to Fossetts with her and help to organise things. It was wonderful to see her foster mother regaining her old strength and energy, but a challenge to prevent the older woman from taking on too much too soon, she reflected ruefully.

Birdie smiled at Misty as she came down into the hall, but her bright blue eyes had an anxious light. 'It's your father...he's waiting in the sitting room.'

Both dismay and surprise assailed Misty. 'Oliver Sargent...he's come here?'

'It's to his credit that he has come to see you,' the older woman pointed out gently. 'Try to be equally generous.'

Torn between curiosity and discomfiture, Misty was as stiff as a plank of wood when she entered the room. The older man had lost weight since their last meeting and the

lines of strain on his features aged him. He bore little re-
semblance to the opinionated and self-important man she
recalled from that weekend in Scotland and simply looked
tired and ill-at-ease.

'But for Leone, I wouldn't have come,' Oliver Sargent
confessed.

Her eyes widened in sharp disconcertion. 'Leone?'

'He encouraged me to visit. I wasn't sure that you'd be
willing to see me.'

'Please sit down.' Belatedly, Misty recalled her manners.

In the strained silence, he took a seat and continued, 'I
imagine that you would first like me to tell you about my
relationship with your mother.'

'Yes.' Misty was relieved that he had taken the lead on
that subject.

'When we met, Carrie was only twenty-one but already
married and a parent,' Oliver said with a sigh. 'Once she
started classes at the university she was mixing with her
own age group and she soon regretted tying herself down
to an older man.'

'Were you *ever* in love with her?' Misty asked tightly.

'I was fond of her, but even then I was engaged to
Jenny. However, Jenny was at home several hundred miles
away,' he told her with a speaking grimace. 'I won't lie…I
saw my affair with Carrie as being a safe outlet for both
of us. I didn't appreciate that nothing is ever that simple
until it was too late.'

'And when was that?'

'Our relationship ended when your mother admitted that
she was pregnant. She believed that she had conceived by
her husband,' the older man said wryly. 'It was only when
he discovered through a blood test after you and your twin
had been born that you were not his kids that the truth
came out.'

'That news must have come as quite a shock to you too,' Misty said rather drily.

'Yes, particularly as Carrie then fled the marital home and arrived on my doorstep with her suitcases. Even though our relationship had been over for months, she expected us to take up where we had left off. It was a ghastly mess for everyone concerned. I didn't love her. I felt trapped. I was twenty-two and I wasn't ready to be a father either. I refused to go to the hospital with her to see you. My biggest fear at the time was that my parents or Jenny might find out what I'd been up to,' Oliver admitted with grim regret. 'When your mother realised how I felt, she moved out. I gave her a considerable amount of money and I never saw or heard from her again.'

'So you didn't see either me or my sister as babies.' That and the knowledge that he had at least offered her mother financial help somewhat eased Misty's desire to sit in harsh judgement over him. She could understand how he must have felt. He might have been slick enough to embark on what he had seen as a convenient affair with a married woman, but he had been far too young to handle the fall-out from a destroyed marriage, a woman as needy as her mother had been and instant fatherhood.

'Your sister…I believe she was adopted?' He gave her an awkward look of enquiry.

Misty confessed that she had no idea where her twin was and he subsided again. Nancy bustling in with a tray of tea created a welcome diversion.

'I *do* appreciate your coming here,' Misty said when they were alone again. 'I also like the fact that you've been honest.'

'This past week telling the truth has become a new habit of mine…' The older man wore a weary air of self-mocking acceptance. 'I've been trying to sort out the mess I've made of my life and Jenny's, but right now she's not willing to listen and I can't blame her. Before this, she was always there for me…'

'And now she's not?' Misty recalled the press revelations concerning his secret country love-nest. She had been relieved for Leone's sake that her father's brief affair with Battista had not become public knowledge, but she was not surprised that his marriage was in serious trouble.

'No…but I hope that that will change.' The haunted look in his eyes stirred genuine compassion in Misty, for he had already lost so much. In the space of weeks, he had gone from being a powerful man, fêted and flattered wherever he went, to being the target of distaste, condemnation and cruel amusement. But she sensed that the loss of Jenny might break him as nothing else might have done.

'When all the fuss has died down, I'd like to get to know you…if you're willing,' her father said levelly. 'But if you think it's a little late in the day for us to become acquainted, I'll understand.'

It was over an hour before he departed, for once the more sensitive points had been broached and dealt with Misty felt free to ask him other questions. He admitted that he had felt appallingly guilty for years afterwards at having taken the easy way out rather than offering her mother the ongoing emotional support that she had needed. He was leaving when Misty took a deep breath and asked him if he would like to come to her wedding.

He froze in surprise. 'Are you willing to have me there? I would like to see the ceremony. I'd keep a very low profile,' he promised with an eagerness that surprised and touched her.

Her first proper meeting with her father left Misty with a great deal to think about, but she was kept busy by the numerous last-minute checks that she felt that she had to make on the wedding arrangements. Early evening, she watched the florist and her assistants decorate the church on the outskirts of town and she could not initially understand why her spirits were so low. She loved Leone, didn't she? Loved him like crazy, so why was she suddenly suffering from a feeling of immense guilt?

Her hands shook as she attempted to position a tall, graceful lily with the same precision as the other women. All right, Leone didn't love her, but he wanted to do the best he could for their child and he did find her very attractive. But was that enough...was that really fair to either him *or* her? The horrid parallels between her own situation and the sad little story her father had told her earlier in the day were working on her conscience and her pride. Wasn't she now doing what her own mother had done?

Carrie had run to Oliver Sargent hoping that he would be willing to take responsibility for her and her twin babies. He had not been willing because he had not cared enough for her mother. Did she despise the older man for that honest confession? Or did she concede that he had probably made the right decision in opting not to offer marriage to a woman with whom he had only had a casual affair? Yet, even knowing that Leone was not in love with her, *she* was planning to allow *him* to go ahead and make her his wife...

That was wrong, absolutely wrong, Misty concluded, perspiration dampening her skin as she reached that agonising decision. Leaving the church, she got back into Birdie's car to drive home, her imagination focused on a frightening and wounding image of what such a marriage might be like a couple of years down the road. What would they have to share but the baby? He would get bored. He would live to regret sacrificing his freedom for a principle. He might even come to *hate* her...

She could not bear that idea. She needed to be strong. She *had* to talk to him before they both made the biggest mistake of their lives. He had been abroad on business since the day after she had agreed to marry him. His absence had made it so much easier for her to refuse to face what she was doing to him. But Leone was staying the night at the Belstone House Hotel and she would go over there to see him once he had checked in.

However, she turned into the driveway at Fossetts and was taken aback to see both Leone's and Flash's sports cars parked at opposing ends of the gravel fronting the old house. Flash strode out to greet her with an accusing look. 'Why didn't you warn Leone that I was going to give you away at the altar tomorrow?'

'I wanted to surprise him.' Pale as death, Misty muttered, 'But I may have dragged you up here on a wild-goose chase because I think I'm going to call off the wedding—'

'You've got cold feet…that's all,' Flash told her, unimpressed. 'You're nuts about him—'

'Tell me something honestly…' Misty studied her foster brother. 'If you had a one-night stand and got the woman pregnant, would you want to marry her?'

'Hell, no!' Flash exclaimed with a revealing shudder.

'Then *why* should Leone?'

Flash looked aghast at the connection she had made. But with a tight, hurting look of acceptance on her face, Misty went indoors, struggling to muster the courage to do what she felt was right even while her foolish heart was hammering just at the prospect of seeing Leone a few hours earlier than she had expected.

She could hear Nancy and Birdie chattering in the kitchen. Leone was in the sitting room. As she entered he sprang upright, his breathtaking smile flashing across his lean, bronzed features, his usual aspect of forbidding cool entirely put to flight. Connecting with his clear dark golden eyes, she felt her knees turn to jelly and her mouth run dry. Striving to regain control of herself, she went rigid when he closed his arms round her.

'*Dio mio*…I thought this week would *never* end,' Leone groaned feelingly. 'I couldn't stay away from you one minute longer. If you hadn't come back, I was going to drive over to the church.'

'Look…er…could we go out into the garden?' Misty asked jerkily. 'I don't want us to be interrupted—'

'Neither do I, *amore*.' Leone strolled over to the French windows to unlock them.

Misty stared at him; hungry eyes roaming over his chiselled profile, the sleek, elegant flow of his lean, powerful body as he moved. Then she shut her eyes tight in anger at her own weakness, hating the idea that she might not be strong enough to give up her hold on the man that she loved even though it seemed to her that that was the only sensible and fair thing to do.

'I want to call off the wedding…' Misty stated with driven abruptness, her voice sounding thin and harsh.

In the act of reaching out to unlock the door, Leone glanced back at her with a stunned light in his eyes. 'What did you say?'

'I'm sorry…but I don't think I should marry you,' Misty told him tightly. 'It wouldn't be right for either of us.'

CHAPTER ELEVEN

THE ghastly silence dragged.

Leone had turned very pale, his bone structure set taut beneath his olive skin. He stared at her in visible disbelief, a frown lodged between his brows as if he was having difficulty in understanding what she had just said.

'Let's go outside before someone comes in,' Misty urged, cringing at the risk of Birdie joining them with some chirpy reference to the wedding while she herself was already questioning the plunge she had taken. Having spoken those words, there could be no going back, no thinking better of what she had believed she ought to do, she registered fearfully.

'Sì…' In agreement, Leone sent a blind seeking hand travelling over the multi-paned French door in apparent search for the key he had been about to turn a minute earlier.

'I know this must've come as a bit of a shock to you—'

'A bit of a shock?' Leone repeated, his Sicilian accent very thick, lean brown fingers still wandering over the door but nowhere near the keyhole. 'You jilting me?'

'I'm *not* jilting you!' Misty gasped with tears of pain stinging her eyes and her throat closing over. 'I'm *trying* to do what's right and fair—'

'*Accidenti*…don't feed me bull like that!' Leone fielded hoarsely. 'I'm not a little kid.'

'You're only marrying me because I'm pregnant and you're going to end up hating me for it,' Misty condemned chokily.

Leone did not seem to be listening to her. He continued

to stare at her in as much apparent shock as if she had pulled a knife on him. There was no gold in the fixed gaze of his stunning eyes, only darkness. 'It's Flash…isn't it?' His rich dark drawl had a slight tremor. 'At the eleventh hour you've realised that you've always loved him—'

Misty was in a state of bewilderment, for Leone was reacting with a much greater degree of shock than she could ever have expected from so self-assured a male. 'Flash has got nothing to do with this—'

'You can get over him,' Leone informed her grittily, his strong jawline clenching. 'No guy in love with you would agree to give you away when you married another man.'

As someone rattled the doorknob from the hall, Misty fled over to the French windows to unlock them. Throwing them wide, she hurried out into the fresh air and struggled to make sense of what Leone was saying to her. Negotiating a path round the ride-on mower sitting parked, she spun round to face him again.

His whole attention was nailed to her with relentless force. 'I'm willing to wait until you come to terms with that. I see no reason why we should cancel the wedding…'

'Leone…I'm not and I've never been in love with Flash,' Misty stated in frustration. 'Yes, he fancied me for a while a few years back and it strained our friendship, but he's got over that now…it was just a phase. He's like my brother.'

Leone stared at her in silence, hard cheekbones prominent, fierce dark eyes glued to her pale, anxious face. 'Then why?' he almost whispered, but every word was underscored by raw-edged emotion. '*Why* have you changed your mind about marrying me?'

'Do you honestly believe that a shotgun marriage is likely to make you happy?' Misty demanded painfully. 'It was my fault that I even *got* pregnant and I know you haven't said a word about that, but you're only human.

Sooner or later, you're going to be thinking that and resenting me for it—'

'No,' Leone slotted in fiercely. 'You're talking nonsense
and this is *not* a shotgun marriage—'

'How can you say that?'

'Because…' Leone snatched in a ragged breath, dark
colour scoring his high cheekbones as he focused on her
with strained eyes of appeal. 'Because I would have asked
you to marry me anyway. Because I was bloody *grateful*
when I realised you were carrying my baby as it gave me
a second chance I wouldn't have got from you any other
way. Because I screwed up every way there was but I do
love you!'

Paralysed by that emotional speech, which carried not a
shade of his usual formidable cool, Misty stared back at
him in total shock, her heart thumping so fast and hard
she felt faint. 'You…you *love* me?'

'I came here to tell you that tonight. I didn't want to
say it on the phone last week because that's not romantic…and I would've said it the night I proposed if I hadn't
felt so threatened by seeing you wrapped round Flash. The
trouble *is*…' Leone paused in that halting flood of charged
explanation to say with a defensive air of masculine discomfiture '…I haven't done this before and, even though
I knew saying it might help, I just couldn't bring myself
to say it…'

'That you loved me?' Misty prompted helpfully.

'You might have laughed and said you didn't believe
me after the way I'd treated you…and I just couldn't work
out how to say it convincingly.' At that point, Leone made
a sudden movement towards her and fell over the ride-on
mower.

And that was the instant when Misty knew beyond a
doubt that Leone really really meant every word he had
just said, for if he could fail to notice a three foot tall

mower in his path, he was a definite lost cause to love. As he picked himself up with a profound aspect of incredulity at the size of the object he had tripped over, a hysterical giggle almost made it out of her throat. But she hastily sealed her lip for she had never loved him more than she loved him at that moment for being clumsy and uncool but very, very human. Even thinking of him having feared a derisive response to his declaration of love squeezed her heartstrings tight. Any desire to giggle had vanished and she was just on fire with love and sympathy for him.

'I'm convinced,' Misty mumbled shakily.

'I really thought I was *never* going to get you back… The baby was a miracle to me too and for you to say that it was your fault that that life-saving development took place…' Leone loosed a shaken laugh at that concept, dark golden eyes pinned to her with disbelief. 'Do you know why I couldn't protect you that weekend?'

Misty shook her head, joy beginning to unfurl inside her and take wings.

'I'm the bright spark who deliberately chose to leave the condoms behind in London because I believed that that would prevent me from dragging you into the nearest bed,' Leone admitted with a rueful light of self-mockery in his beautiful eyes that released crazy butterflies in her tummy. 'I took the risk. I took the risk knowing what I was doing because I couldn't resist you and I no more regret that risk than I could *ever* regret the consequences.'

'I believe you…' Misty felt pure *femme fatale* at that moment and her slim shoulders went back with pride. There he was, all gorgeous and sophisticated, but she had been too much temptation for him: he had been scared enough to try and control his own libido by doing something utterly crazy. She had been afraid that he might have slept with her that weekend just because she'd been available. The discovery that he had been as caught up and controlled by the overwhelming attraction between them as she had been freed her for ever from that fear.

'I swear that if you marry me tomorrow, you'll never live to regret it, *amore*.' His anxious gaze rested on her and then his eyes veiled, a tiny muscle tugging at the corner of his strained mouth. 'You don't need to share a bed with me if you don't want to…OK?'

'OK…' Misty was falling victim to fascination, her nicer side telling her she ought to confess that she loved him too, but her darker side keen not to miss out on discovering what lengths Leone might go to in his determination to persuade her to marry him.

Her Sicilian bridegroom received that agreement without perceptible surprise or objection. 'I know that it's likely to be a long time before you feel that you can trust me again—'

'We made love last week,' Misty reminded him.

'But that was like a comfort thing for you, wasn't it?' Leone muttered darkly. 'You had had a very stressful day and you didn't really know what you wanted from me that night—'

'Is that what you thought?' Misty was wounded on his behalf.

'I was just thankful you came to me…' Leone shot her a wry look. 'I'll take whatever you're willing to give on any terms. Haven't you worked that out yet?'

Misty was stunned by that assurance. She closed the distance between them and wrapped her arms tight round him, melting into the lean, hard strength of him and drinking in his achingly familiar scent with a deep sense of coming home where she belonged. 'The terms will be very easy,' she swore shakily into his shoulder. 'We're definitely getting married tomorrow. There's no way you're getting your freedom now.'

'I don't want it, *amore mio*,' Leone breathed thickly, a

slight tremor shaking through his big powerful frame. 'I felt like the roof had fallen in on me when you said the wedding was off. I couldn't handle it…I just didn't know what to say, what to do—'

'I'm so sorry I said it now,' she confided guiltily. 'It was just listening to Oliver talk today about how it had been with him and my mother. He didn't love her and, when I thought about it, I felt he was right not to let himself feel forced into continuing the relationship out of guilt because what did they have in common? All they had was physical attraction—'

Leone claimed a fierce, devouring kiss and then just held her tight before walking her in her still shell-shocked emotional state round the corner of the house to his car and unlocking the passenger door for her. 'We've got a hell of a lot more going for us than that, *bella mia*.'

'Like what?' she said ungrammatically when he swung in beside her.

Leone fired the engine into a throaty purr and turned to look at her with candid golden eyes. 'I can't live without you in my life.'

'Oh…' Misty surrendered to feeling happy. 'Where are we going?'

'I don't know but right now I feel like I might be scared enough to sit on your doorstep all night in case you change your mind about the wedding again,' Leone admitted half under his breath.

'I won't…I promise!' she exclaimed.

He parked in a layby down the road and threw back his proud dark head to study her with intent interest. When she thought about it she realised that he always looked at her that way and when she smiled, he smiled as if he couldn't help himself. All along his love had been there for her to see if only she had had the faith and the confidence to recognise it.

'I think I fell in love with you long before you ever signed that crazy contract. I was obsessed by you,' Leone confided with a rueful laugh. 'I was up at Brewsters every other week when I had no reason to visit, watching you every second you were in the same room—'

'So that *wasn't* my imagination.'

'And all the time I was thinking you were greedy and calculating and sort of hating and lusting after you simultaneously,' Leone groaned, shooting her dismayed face a glance of guilty regret. 'I wanted to believe bad stuff about you then. It put a barrier between us and I needed that barrier, but once I began spending time with you all that went pear-shaped on me overnight.'

'Did it?'

'Right from the start there was this weird sense of connecting…and then that first kiss…no kiss was ever that explosive for me! I couldn't keep my hands off you after that—'

'I would probably have died of disappointment if you had.' Misty was hanging onto his every word, silvery grey eyes clinging to his darkly handsome features as though her life did indeed depend on him. 'That wild attraction was very mutual but I hated you too at the beginning.'

Leone tensed and paled. 'I was a total bastard, so I can't blame you for that,' he acknowledged hoarsely. 'But I tried so *hard* to stop what I had begun with the press to protect you, and when I failed I knew what hell felt like. There you were suffering and I'd brought it on you and wrecked what I might have had with you.'

She reached for his coiled fingers. 'I was very hurt but you were wonderful—'

'Some kind of wonderful,' Leone breathed with harsh self-derision. 'I was panicking. I knew I would lose you the instant I told you the truth—'

'Is that why you asked me to move in with you?'

'I thought a marriage proposal after one weekend would make you lift the phone to call a psychiatrist for me. *Dio mio*…didn't you feel my desperation?'

'No, there was no mower for you to trip over and I was in deep shock,' Misty pointed out. 'But if you'd dragged out the L word then…the love bit, I think I'd have stopped a little longer to listen.'

He linked his fingers with hers, beautiful golden eyes tender and warm and lodged with flattering intensity on her. 'You said you were scared of me and that really tore me up. I knew I had asked for that, but it would have seemed like a *very* bad joke if I'd tried to persuade you then that I loved you after what I'd done to you.'

'No, if the woman is *in* love she might consider a love plea in those circumstances a bad joke at first,' Misty told him with immense superiority. 'She would think things like, I bet he doesn't really mean it…but then later when she had calmed down she would think about it more and maybe start making excuses for him having behaved like a toerag. Within the space of a few days she would be feeling much more forgiving and understanding.'

A bewildered frownline had lodged between Leone's winged ebony brows. 'Is that a fact?'

Misty nodded, a helpless smile building on her lush pink mouth. 'So you missed your best chance not going for the L word that day—'

'Are you saying that you love me?' Leone muttered thickly.

'Oh, yes…loads and loads. I was only trying to call off our wedding earlier because I felt so guilty about marrying you when *you* didn't love *me*.'

'You love me…and you still dumped me?' Leone seemed to be in shock again. 'And you call *me* ruthless?'

Misty waited for him to come to terms with her revelation.

Suddenly he was trying to haul her into his arms but there really wasn't room in the low-slung sports car for that kind of caper, so he tugged her out of the car, braced her up against the passenger door with feverish impatience and kissed her until she drowned in his hungry passion.

'I love you so much. I don't deserve that you love me too…' he muttered raggedly.

As a car horn cheekily sounded from a passing vehicle, Leone jerked back from her with a groan and settled her back into the car again. From his pocket he withdrew a tiny box embellished with a famous jewellers' logo. 'I also came over tonight to give you this.'

Holding her breath, Misty opened the box on a breath-taking diamond and sapphire ring. He took her hand and slid the beautiful engagement ring onto her finger. She watched the jewels catch fire in the sunlight and gave him a huge appreciative smile. 'It's gorgeous.'

'And then there's this…your wedding present.' Leone set a very large and very old ornate iron key on her lap.

Dreamy eyes still shining from the gift of the ring, Misty gazed down at the key in bewilderment. She knew some people collected old keys and, as old keys went, she supposed it was a top-notch find and she tried to sound appropriately impressed. 'It looks so old…it's just… er…fascinating—'

'Castle Eyrie is yours,' Leone murmured silkily.

Misty dredged her attention from the key and focused on him, wide-eyed. 'You *bought* the castle?'

'Why not?'

'You *hated* it!' Misty gasped helplessly. 'You said it was falling apart and it would be a money pit for the fool that bought it—'

'I can afford a money pit, and by the time the restoration is complete it will be a prime piece of real estate.' Perceptible dark colour underscoring his fabulous cheekbones, Leone screened his gorgeous eyes. 'You fell in love with Castle Eyrie and I feel it has some special memories for us,' he confided half under his breath. 'I bought most of the contents as well and persuaded Murdo to stay on in a supervisory capacity—'

Misty launched herself at him and locked her arms round his neck as best she could in the confines of the car. Eyes bright with love and tenderness and glowing appreciation, she told him he was the most romantic man she had ever met and he groaned out loud, but she could see he was pleased that she was so delighted.

'Just don't expect me to take up fishing,' he warned her with a shudder.

He really had to take her home again then. It was the evening before their wedding and she was planning on an early night. When Leone walked back into Fossetts and greeted Flash with an easy smile and not the slightest hint of unease, the very last of her concerns vanished.

At eleven the following morning, Misty walked down the aisle on Flash's arm and a collective gasp of appreciation filled the church as she came into view with her bridesmaids, Clarice and an old schoolfriend, following in her wake. Her copper hair fell in a shining curtain of silk to her bare shoulders while her green brocade sleeveless top hugged her slender curves and the full ivory silk skirt flattered her still narrow waist and swept to the floor like a ballgown. The same wonderful diamonds she had worn to the movie première glittered at her throat and her ears, for Leone had brought them down from London for her.

Misty had eyes for no one but Leone, who was watching her approach the altar with a satisfyingly transfixed expression on his lean, strong face. He was drop-dead gorgeous in his well-cut dark suit, but it was the look of love in his level dark golden gaze that made her heart race the fastest. After the simple ceremony, having signed the register, they walked together back down the aisle and she took time out from her own bubbling happiness to smile at her father, who was seated in a rear pew.

'I never thanked you for encouraging Oliver to visit me,' she whispered to Leone on the steps while the photos were being taken.

His arm tightened round her. 'He didn't need much encouragement, *bella mia*.'

Flash grabbed her hand before she could climb into the limousine and hissed, 'Who's the bridesmaid with the black hair?'

Misty gave him an amused glance and followed his gaze to where her friend and former employee, Clarice, stood flirting like mad with Leone's best man, a handsome Italian businessman, who seemed equally taken with the bubbly brunette. 'Her name's Clarice. She likes country music…and guys over thirty.'

'You're kidding?'

Misty grinned. 'Sorry, I'm not.'

Leone reached for her hand in the limo and gave her a slashing, self-mocking smile that turned her susceptible heart inside out. 'Until last night, I was so jealous of Flash I wanted to kill him every time I saw him!'

'I know…and I'm glad you don't feel like that any more. Like Birdie, he's family.'

'You look ravishing, *amore*.' He feasted his attention on her and his brilliant eyes smouldered gold before his black lashes dropped low to conceal them, a hint of tension tautening his strong bone structure. 'I should mention that you're going to have a special surprise today.'

'What kind of surprise?'

'I'm not at liberty to tell you, but I had very little to do with arranging it.'

'You sound like a bloke baling out in advance of a

crash.' Misty studied him anxiously. 'What are you keeping from me?'

'Nothing you need to worry about,' Leone swore in vehement retreat. 'I just want this to be the very happiest day of your life.'

And he thought that the surprise might not be a happy one?

'Is it something to do with my twin?' she asked right out of the blue.

He tensed. 'No.'

'You've invited all your ex-girlfriends to the reception?'

'Do I look like a man with a death wish?'

Reassured, Misty nestled under his arm. 'By the way, when did you break up with that blonde television actress?'

'The night I called her, "Misty,"' Leone admitted grudgingly.

Misty was tickled pink by that admission. 'And when was that?'

'Is this an interrogation?'

'Yeah...and if you don't tell me, Leone...how is this going to be the happiest day of my life?' Misty teased in a die-away voice of reproach.

'It was a few weeks before the contract I made you sign.'

Wreathed in smiles at that ego-boosting confession, Misty pondered what the surprise in store for her might encompass. Far more people were attending the reception than had been at the church, which had not had the capacity for large numbers. By the time she had shaken hands with what felt like five hundred people, most of whom were strangers, she had quite forgotten the matter. Midway through their meal, she glanced across the room and saw a young blonde woman staring at her and she had one of those faces that seemed to strike a chord of familiarity with Misty. But as their eyes met the other woman looked away with an odd air of discomfiture.

'Who's that blonde sitting beside the hunky dark guy?'

'What *hunky* dark guy?' her bridegroom growled, rising easily to the bait.

Misty giggled. 'They're at that table just inside the door.'

Leone tensed. 'That's Freddy and Jaspar al-Husayn.'

'Friends?'

'Recent acquaintances.' Leone seemed to be picking his words with quite unnecessary care. 'He's the Crown Prince of Quamar—'

'They're like...*royalty*?' Misty gasped. 'I don't remember seeing them earlier—'

'They arrived late. She's English. We'll talk to them later—'

'Leave me out of it,' Misty told him with a slight grimace. 'I wouldn't know what to say to a princess!'

Leone shot her a startled look. 'Freddy struck me as being very friendly—'

'I'm sure.' Misty was unimpressed by that accolade, thinking that men were not the best judges of beautiful blondes. 'But I've never met anyone royal before and I'd be scared of putting my feet in it.'

As the afternoon advanced she drifted round the dance floor secure in Leone's arms and cocooned in a dreaming daze of contentment. When it was time for her to go and get changed to head for their honeymoon in Sicily, she went upstairs to the suite set aside for their use. Her bridesmaids, who had promised to follow her up, failed to show and she had just finished donning an elegant blue shift dress when someone knocked on the door.

She was taken aback to find herself facing, or rather looking down at, Freddy al-Husayn, who was not very tall.

'May I come in and talk to you?' the other woman asked with an uncertain air.

Perplexed, Misty stepped back.

'I'm the surprise that your husband wasn't too sure he wanted you to have,' Freddy explained in an apologetic rush. 'He said he didn't want you to be upset, and when he explained how my father once turned you away from my home and told you that I would want nothing to do with you, I was *so* ashamed and angry. But at the same time I was overjoyed that, four years ago, you wanted that contact and I'm hoping you'll feel the same way now.'

Silenced by that bewildering conversational opening, Misty simply stared, a frownline forming between her brows.

'We had the same mother...' Freddy said awkwardly. 'But I'm afraid I'm not your twin, I'm only a half-sister. Jaspar and Leone both thought I should wait until you came back from your honeymoon, but that's weeks away and I'm not good at being patient when I've been looking for you for so long!'

'You're my sister...' Stunned as she was by that real-isation, Misty immediately found herself staring just as Freddy had stared several hours earlier. 'Oh, what a *wonderful* surprise! What on earth was Leone thinking about when he asked you to wait until after our honeymoon?' she exclaimed.

From that point on, it was a challenge to see who could say the most the fastest before the other interrupted with some question or comment. Words and explanations flowed at the speed of light. Misty laughed at the reality that her big sister was smaller than she was, and listened with deep pleasure to the news that it was eighteen months since Freddy had begun searching for her.

'It's only forty-eight hours since we found out where you lived but Jaspar didn't think just before your wedding was a very good time to confront you with a sister you mightn't even *know* existed!' Freddy rattled on ruefully. 'So he approached Leone first in London and swore him to secrecy because I wanted to be the first to tell you *who* I was…I didn't want it coming from anyone else.'

No wonder Leone had been apprehensive, Misty reflected fondly as she recalled her own angry, defensive reaction to his offer to help her trace one of her sisters. It made her smile too to think of their husbands conspiring to protect both of them as far as possible from the risk of hurt or rejection.

'My sister's a princess…but you're so normal!' Laughing, but with tears of happiness in her eyes, Misty grasped Freddy's hand in hers and they hugged, each of them knowing in that intrinsically female fashion that they had found a friend as well as a sister.

They were getting on like a house on fire when Leone appeared with Jaspar only a step in his wake. Misty only had to see Jaspar smile in relief at his wife's happy face to lose all fear of his exalted status. Leone and Misty went downstairs to say goodbye to their guests, but Jaspar and Freddy accompanied them to the airport. Having been re-united for such a short time, the two sisters found it hard to part so soon afterwards.

It was evening when Leone and Misty arrived at his country villa in the lush fertile hills above the town of Enna. A grand arched entrance embellished by tall gates opened off the steep winding road, leading them through a grove of olive and citrus trees before the beautiful gardens came into the view. In the centre sat the Villa Fortuna, tall, shuttered windows cast open now that the heat of the day had passed, tawny, weathered walls gold in the light of the setting sun.

'It's idyllic,' Misty whispered, thrilled to be seeing the house where Leone had grown up.

An hour later a light refreshing breeze fluttered the curtains in the bedroom as he pulled her close and she trembled at the touch and the feel of him. 'It's been the best day of my life,' she muttered shakily.

'It can still get better, *bella mia*.' A very masculine smile of promise on his lean, darkly handsome features, he drew her down onto the bed, watched her hair stream across the pillow like rich copper silk, and he gazed down at her with unashamed possessive intensity. 'I used to picture you like this in this room…in my bed.'

Misty curved an equally possessive hand to his stubborn jawline and looked up into his stunning golden eyes. 'Just one little question…did you *really* settle Birdie's mortgage for purely altruistic reasons?'

He tensed and then flashed her a rueful smile of breathtaking charm. 'Maybe fifty-fifty. I couldn't bear to think of you struggling to keep up the payments. But if I'd admitted that it would have been the kiss of death to my hopes of winning you back. When I saw Flash waiting down in the car park for you…it was probably the very *worst* moment of my life—'

'Honestly?'

He splayed gentle fingers against her still-flat stomach and surveyed her with tender eyes of loving satisfaction. 'But finding out about our baby was the equivalent of being thrown a lifebelt when I was drowning. I adore you, Signora Andracchi—'

Misty leant up to him and claimed his wide, sensual mouth for herself and the sweet, drugging heat of her own flaring response took over. He tasted her with a ragged groan and stopped to tell her how happy he was, only to be dragged back down into her arms and told that there would be plenty of time to talk later…

*   *   *

Eleven months on, in the atmospheric nursery at Castle Eyrie, Misty checked on their son, Connor. He was fast asleep. He had soft black curls and big trusting blue eyes and, at three months old, he was fascinating his adoring parents more with every passing day. Indeed, Flash had warned them that they were at risk of getting a little boring on the subject of his godchild.

It had been an incredibly busy and eventful year for all of them. Jaspar and Freddy had come to stay with them several times during Misty's pregnancy and Leone and Misty had since spent a fabulous vacation in the desert kingdom of Quamar. It was fortunate that Leone and Jaspar got on so well because Misty and Freddy pretty much left the men to their own devices when they got together. In fact developing a close relationship with her newfound sister and getting to know her nephews, Ben and Kareem, had given Misty a great deal of pleasure.

Just one thing marred that pleasure for both women, and that was their complete failure to discover any further information about Misty's twin. As time went on, it seemed less and less likely to Misty that she would ever trace her younger sister.

The hospital records of Shannon's birth still existed but the agency record of her adoption was missing—a fact which Leone considered suspicious, as those records *had* been intact when Misty had first attempted to contact her sibling. He believed that someone had since chosen to remove those records. He even thought that that brief letter of wounding rejection that Misty had received four years earlier might not even have been written by her sister. It had taken Leone to look at that letter and point out that the average teenager would scarcely express herself in such a guarded and very formal manner.

Suppressing her regret that she had celebrated her twenty-third birthday without coming any closer to finding her twin, Misty kissed her son goodnight and left the nursery. There was nothing chilly about Castle Eyrie now, for underfloor heating had been installed. The linen cupboards rejoiced in serried ranks of top-quality bedlinen and the bathrooms were splendid affairs. Every piece of antique furniture gleamed with the evocative sheen and scent of beeswax and Murdo, who flatly refused to retire even though he was seventy-five, took a brandy nightcap to bed every evening.

Misty loved the castle and Leone had grown to love it too, for when they were in the Highlands they got to spend the maximum amount of time relaxing together. A month earlier, her father and Jenny had spent a weekend with them. Oliver had managed to mend his marriage, but had only recently come through the stressful humiliating enquiries that he had had to withstand over his conduct during his time as a politician. However, her father was now putting his skills as an organiser to good use by working for a mental health charity. Although it was very much a backroom kind of job and unpaid, he had been extremely grateful that someone was prepared to give him the chance to work again. He was a changed man, a much more likeable man and he was very taken with Connor. Birdie was another one of Connor's keen admirers and was a regular visitor when she could tear herself away from her beloved garden at Fossetts.

As Misty counted all the blessings of her life with a dreamy smile, she concentrated on the most important person in it next to Connor: Leone. She just adored him, but she kept him on his toes too. He spent far less time abroad on business than he had when they had first met, and for her birthday he had presented her with a beautiful diamond eternity ring engraved with her name and his.

She was wearing a sassy ice-blue nightdress and her copper hair was loose round her shoulders just the way

Leone liked her to wear it. Her face warmed at the wanton heat already bubbling through her at the thought of his passion. Leone was peeling off his shirt when she entered their bedroom. He was an arresting sight and her mouth ran dry.

'Connor was asleep, wasn't he?' Leone teased her huskily. 'I *told* you I'd already checked on him.'

'I just like to check for myself.' Misty was embarrassed to admit that sometimes she just liked to look into her baby son's cot and glory in the sheer wonder of his existence. But, having been reassured that she would have no trouble in conceiving a second time, she wanted to wait a couple of years before she had another child.

'Come here...' Leone urged with smouldering dark golden eyes.

Heartbeat quickening, Misty looked back at him with a deep feminine appreciation undimmed by eleven months of marriage. He had always been gorgeous but he was just *so* male and sexy as well. She still woke up beside him some mornings and marvelled that he was all hers. She glided into his arms like a homing pigeon.

He curved her slender body to his lean, muscular length with a roughened sound of satisfaction and held her close. 'We'll go back to Sicily for our anniversary trip next month, *amore mio*.'

'Bliss,' she sighed in delight, thinking that life with Leone just seemed to be one long series of magical treats and grateful that he wasn't the workaholic that she had once feared he might be.

'And as a special favour, you'll bake mouth-watering *nucatoli* and *pasta ciotti* for me,' Leone said silkily. 'Just the way you did that first day. I found that very sexy—'

'*Sexy?* Me baking cakes?' Misty gasped. 'When I write my best selling book on how to trap a Sicilian tycoon and keep him happy, I'll be sure to mention that the good old home-cooking angle really hits the weirdest spot with some guys!'

In mock fury, Leone tumbled her down onto the bed and she curled up in a giggling heap. 'Of course, there is the bedroom angle too!'

Her husband came down beside her and gazed down into her laughing face with vibrant amusement. 'You're a hussy, *bella mia*—'

'But you love me loads,' Misty whispered, arching up to meet the devouring heat of his sensual mouth with a sigh of pleasure.

They both heard the phone by the bed ring. They both ignored it. But it went on and on and on and eventually Leone pulled back from her with an anguished groan of frustration and swept up the receiver.

'No...no, of course it's not too late to call us,' Leone swore and then he stiffened, a look of surprise tightening is strong bone structure, causing his dark, expressive brows to rise above golden eyes that were now focused with keen concentration.

'What's wrong?' Misty hissed anxiously. 'Who is it?'

'Birdie...' Leone turned to look at her. 'She says that your twin sister has been at Fossetts asking for you...'

In shock, Misty stared at him, and then as the news sank in she was gripped by such a fierce surge of joy and excitement that she could neither think straight nor put her feelings into actual words...

If you enjoyed what you just read,
then we've got an offer you can't resist!

Take 2 bestselling love stories FREE!

Plus get a FREE surprise gift!

Clip this page and mail it to Harlequin Reader Service®

IN U.S.A.	IN CANADA
3010 Walden Ave.	P.O. Box 609
P.O. Box 1867	Fort Erie, Ontario
Buffalo, N.Y. 14240-1867	L2A 5X3

YES! Please send me 2 free Harlequin Presents® novels and my free surprise gift. After receiving them, if I don't wish to receive anymore, I can return the shipping statement marked cancel. If I don't cancel, I will receive 6 brand-new novels every month, before they're available in stores! In the U.S.A., bill me at the bargain price of $3.57 plus 25¢ shipping & handling per book and applicable sales tax, if any*. In Canada, bill me at the bargain price of $4.24 plus 25¢ shipping & handling per book and applicable taxes**. That's the complete price and a savings of at least 10% off the cover prices—what a great deal! I understand that accepting the 2 free books and gift places me under no obligation ever to buy any books. I can always return a shipment and cancel at any time. Even if I never buy another book from Harlequin, the 2 free books and gift are mine to keep forever.

106 HDN DNTZ
306 HDN DNT2

Name	(PLEASE PRINT)	
Address	Apt.#	
City	State/Prov.	Zip/Postal Code

* Terms and prices subject to change without notice. Sales tax applicable in N.Y.

** Canadian residents will be charged applicable provincial taxes and GST.
   All orders subject to approval. Offer limited to one per household and not valid to
   current Harlequin Presents® subscribers.

® are registered trademarks of Harlequin Enterprises Limited.

PRES02   ©2001 Harlequin Enterprises Limited

$ Saving Money $ Has Never Been This Easy!

Just fill out and send in this form from any October, November and December 2002 books and we will send you a coupon booklet worth a total savings of $20.00 off future purchases of Harlequin and Silhouette books in 2003.

Yes! It's that easy!

I accept your incredible offer!
Please send me a coupon booklet:

Name (PLEASE PRINT)

Address   Apt. #

City   State/Prov.   Zip/Postal Code

In a typical month, how many
Harlequin and Silhouette novels do you read?

❏ 0-2   ❏ 3+

097KJKDNC7   097KJKDNDP

Please send this form to:
In the U.S.: Harlequin Books, P.O. Box 9071, Buffalo, NY 14269-9071
In Canada: Harlequin Books, P.O. Box 609, Fort Erie, Ontario L2A 5X3

Allow 4-6 weeks for delivery. Limit one coupon booklet per household. Must be postmarked no later than January 15, 2003.

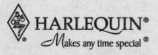

HARLEQUIN®
Makes any time special®

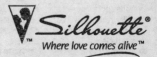

Silhouette®
Where love comes alive™

© 2002 Harlequin Enterprises Limited   PHQ402

International bestselling author

SANDRA MARTON

invites you to attend the

WEDDING *of the* YEAR

Glitz and glamour prevail in this volume
containing a trio of stories in which
three couples meet at a
high society wedding—and
soon find themselves
walking down the aisle!

Look for it in November 2002.

Lindsay Armstrong...
Helen Bianchin...
Emma Darcy...
Miranda Lee...

Some of our bestselling writers are Australians!

Look our for their novels about the Wonder from Down Under—where spirited women win the hearts of Australia's most eligible men.

THE AUSTRALIANS

Coming soon:

THE MARRIAGE RISK
by Emma Darcy
On sale February 2001, Harlequin Presents® #2157

And look out for:

MARRIAGE AT A PRICE
by Miranda Lee
On sale June 2001, Harlequin Presents® #2181

Available wherever Harlequin books are sold.

HARLEQUIN®
Makes any time special ™